WRITTEN BY
D.C. FREEDMAN

Paper in this book is made using 30% post-consumer recycled waste.
Printed and bound by Gasch Printing in Odenton, Maryland, USA.

Cover photo elements ©iStockphoto/lazyllama, ©iStockphoto/svengine
Design and formatting by Jennifer Ferguson.

www.dcfreedman.com

Praise for The Jamie Johnson Series

"You'll read this and want to get out there and play"
STEVEN GERRARD

"Had me flipping the pages faster than lightning"
SPORTS ILLUSTRATED KIDS

"Unlike any book series written in the world"
BRAD FRIEDEL

"I love reading about soccer and it doesn't get
much better than this"
JOE HART

"An inspiring read for all soccer fans"
GARY LINEKER

"Jamie could go all the way"
JERMAIN DEFOE

"Pure class—brings the game to life"
OWEN COYLE

About The
Jamie Johnson Series

The Jamie Johnson Series follows the life of a boy who dreams of being a famous professional soccer player. We first meet Jamie Johnson in fifth grade, and we follow every step of his journey from school all the way through to soccer's biggest stage, the World Cup, and even beyond.

These bestselling novels originated in the United Kingdom, where their author, D.C Freedman, lives. D.C. is thrilled to announce the second book in The Jamie Johnson Series, *School of Skill*, to the United States, which has been adapted exclusively for the American audience. Be sure to check out *Born to Play*, the first chapter in Jamie's journey, and keep an eye out for the next installment of The Jamie Johnson Series—coming soon!

facebook.com/JamieJohnson11
@DCFreedman

About the Author

D.C. FREEDMAN grew up wanting to be a professional soccer player. That didn't happen. But he went on to become a top soccer journalist, personally interviewing the likes of Cristiano Ronaldo, Lionel Messi and David Beckham. He uses his passion and knowledge of the game to write the hugely popular series of Jamie Johnson soccer novels. When he is not writing, D.C. delivers talks and workshops for schools. He discusses his experiences in soccer and his career as a writer, passing on one simple message to kids everywhere: *Go For Your Goals!* D.C. still plays soccer whenever he can.

www.DCFreedman.com

School of
SKILL

**Jamie's heading to Brazil
to learn from the best!**

A NOVEL BY
D.C. FREEDMAN

A press conference is being held at Hawkstone United's stadium.

A sharply dressed man walks through the door and into the room. It is full of photographers and journalists all there to hear what he has to say.

The man sits down at the table and clears his throat. He knows what he is going to say. He spent all of last night preparing these words. He has been preparing for this moment his entire life.

He pulls the microphone towards him and begins to speak.

"I want to say what an honor it is to be managing in the Premier League and, in particular, here at Hawkstone United," he explains.

His voice is cool, crisp, clear and confident.

"This is a dream come true for me."

PART ONE

What Makes You So Special?

Tuesday, April 29th

"Jamie Johnson!" Mr. Pratley shouted, his hot, smelly coffee breath roaring like a dirty hurricane into Jamie's face.

He grabbed Jamie's scribbled line-up of a Hawkstone United team with all his favorite players and, of course, J. Johnson as number 11, the left-winger.

This was far from the first time that Jamie had been caught playing fantasy soccer instead of listening. When it came to soccer, Jamie's brain was like a powerful computer, working out teams, angles, shots and passes... but when it came to listening to Pratley, well, Jamie just seemed to turn off as soon as the man started talking. It drove Pratley wild with rage.

"Do you have you any idea how many kids have been

through this school and claimed that they were going to be a professional soccer player when they grew up? Hundreds... thousands!"

Mr. Pratley was now tearing up Jamie's sheet into as many little pieces as possible. The more he ripped the page into smaller and smaller pieces, the redder his face became and the wider his eyes bulged.

Jamie did not respond. He couldn't. It was taking every ounce of his focus not to burst into laughter. All he could do was stare at the big green booger that was hovering, tantalizingly loose, from the end of Mr. Pratley's nostril. It was a beauty: wet and sticky, yet still hard enough to be absolutely ripe for the picking.

"And of those thousands of kids," Pratley continued, the redness now rising from his face into his big, shiny, balding head, "who ALL thought they were going to be professional soccer players, who ALL thought they were God's gift to the game—just like you no doubt do — have you any idea how many of them did it? How many of them became pro soccer players?"

Jamie shook his head. He noticed the more Pratley was getting worked up and the louder he shouted, the more the booger began to wobble. It was as though it was dancing to the beat of Pratley's anger.

Pratley walked to the front of the classroom and chucked the remnants of Jamie's sheet into the trash. Then he turned and marched back towards Jamie.

The closer he got, the better the view Jamie had of

the booger. It was now doing something amazing. When Pratley breathed out, the booger poked further out of his nose, as if it were waving to the world. And when he breathed in, it returned slightly further back up his nostril. It appeared to be on some kind of invisible string.

"None!!" barked Pratley. "Not one of those kids became professional soccer players! So, I would like you to tell me why you think you are any different."

Jamie looked at his best friend, Alexandra—or, Alex, as everyone knew her—for help. She shook her head. *Don't talk back.* That's what she was signalling with her eyes. And she was right. This was a regular occurrence between Jamie and Mr. Pratley.

For some reason, Jamie had the ability to get under Pratley's skin more than any other kid in the whole school. Normally the kids found it hysterical, but right now, they had reached the danger zone; one more word from Jamie and Pratley just might explode.

Of course there were plenty of things Jamie could have said; lots of arguments he could have put forward to explain why he believed that, one day, he would become a professional soccer player...

He was by far the best player in the school, and he got all his talent from his grandfather, who, had it not been for the injury, would easily have been one of Hawkstone's greatest-ever players. Jamie trained and practiced every single day because he wanted to become not just a professional soccer player but one of the best players in the world...

But he didn't say anything. Alex was right. They both knew that whenever Jamie answered back, it only made Pratley even angrier. The best course of action Jamie could take now would be to say nothing. Nothing at all.

And so Jamie just shrugged his shoulders and stayed quiet.

"Answer me, Johnson!" yelled Pratley. "Or I'll keep you in here for the entire lunch period by yourself. What makes you think you're so special? What makes you think you've got something that all those other kids didn't?"

Pratley's face was now just an inch from Jamie's. The booger was smack bang in front of Jamie's eyes. It was moving in and out of the teacher's nose, perfectly in time with Pratley's pants of fury.

Out of the corner of his eye, Jamie saw Alex turn away. Her body was quivering. She had seen it too, and had started laughing without making any noise.

Jamie could feel it coming inside him too. It was rising up through his body like an unstoppable river from his lungs into his throat, and now it was at his mouth. The laughter could not be controlled for very much longer.

"For the very last time, Johnson! Why do you think you are better than any of them?"

"I don't know..." Jamie finally stuttered. The laughter was already leaking out. He knew he was going to get into trouble anyway, so he thought he might as well make it worth it.

"**Snot** really for me to say!"

The Day of Destiny

"We'll know tomorrow!" shouted Alex, grabbing Jamie by his shirt and dragging him out of lunch.

"Know what?" he asked, laughing as she dragged him along all the way to the auditorium.

"TOMORROW!" she repeated, pushing him face to face with the sheet of paper on the bulletin board that announced their day of destiny.

Teachers vs 6th Grade Students

SOCCER MATCH

....

The date for this game has been confirmed!

Details will be announced at assembly tomorrow.

Jamie stared at the board.

The note was about the soccer game that he had being looking forward to all year, the match between the teachers of Wheatlands Primary School and the sixth grade students. When Jamie first moved to the UK a little over a year ago, he thought it was weird that the school was for first through sixth graders.

But now that he was a sixth grader, on top of the food chain at Wheatlands, Jamie knew this game was going to be huge. Maybe the biggest game of his life.

Jamie and Alex gazed at the Wheatlands Primary School Soccer Trophy. Gleaming like treasure, it stood, as always, in its special cabinet in the auditorium. It remained there for the whole year until, on the day of the game itself, the principal, Mr. Karenza, removed the prize from the cabinet and handed it to the winning captain to lift into the air.

Alex, who had been at Wheatlands since first grade, regaled Jamie with horror stories of the previous sixth graders' embarrassing losses at the hands of the teachers. Even though Alex was already the best goalkeeper in the school by fourth grade, she could only look on helpless from the sidelines as the teachers racked up win after win, year after year.

But this year Jamie and Alex were in sixth grade. Now it was their chance to play and put things right, to finally give the teachers a taste of their own medicine.

They had promised themselves that, in this game, things would be different, that this would be their year.

However, just one look at the wooden board—on which was engraved the results of all the previous matches—spelled out the difficulty of the task that lay ahead.

And it also named the teacher who would be standing in their way.

Teachers vs Sixth Grade Students
GAME RESULTS

Teachers 11–8 Students	Winning Captain: C Pratley
Teachers 6–4 Students	Winning Captain: C Pratley
Teachers 4–4 Students	Match abandoned
Teachers 8–1 Students	Winning Captain: C Pratley
Teachers 7–3 Students	Winning Captain: C Pratley
Teachers 5–2 Students	Winning Captain: C Pratley
Teachers 9–6 Students	Winning Captain: C Pratley
Teachers 5–3 Students	Winning Captain: C Pratley
Teachers 7–6 Students	Winning Captain: C Pratley
Teachers 6–4 Students	Winning Captain: C Pratley
Teachers Students	Winning Captain:

3

10,000 Hours

"Come on," said Alex. "Spit it out."

She and Jamie were walking home from school together, as they did every day, kicking an old soda can between them along the street.

Jamie shook his head. Sometimes, he didn't like to talk. Even to Alex.

"Look," she said. "You always tell me eventually, so why don't we just skip past the silent bit and get to the talking bit?"

Jamie stared at her. Alex constantly surprised and impressed him. It had been the same since the day he met her.

She was one of the only kids in fifth grade that bothered to get to know Jamie when he joined Wheatlands after he moved from the United States. They connected straight away, forging a strong partnership. And, with Jamie being an attacker and Alex being a brilliant goalkeeper, they could practice together every day, challenging each other to reach the highest levels.

Not that Alex was just someone for Jamie to kick around with after school. She was his first true friend in the UK. Somehow, Alex made Jamie feel comfortable no matter what. Often Jamie felt that she knew him better than he knew himself.

"It's that stuff Pratley was saying today," Jamie began, "that I'm no different than all the other kids that wanted to be pro soccer players and didn't make it. I know I was laughing and stuff, but I can't get it out of my head."

"You're not still worried about Pratley, are you?" Alex said. "Just because he's a teacher doesn't mean he knows everything. My dad always says that the people that make the rules aren't any better than the rest of us."

"Yeah," said Jamie, "but what if Pratley's actually right? What if I am no better than the others?"

"OK. So what are you going to do about it?" she responded immediately.

"What?" said Jamie. He was shocked by her abruptness and missed his kick of the can.

"Well, you can either keep worrying about it, thinking you're no better than everyone else, or, if being a pro soccer player really is your dream, you can start making it happen, doing something to give yourself that extra edge."

Jamie smiled at her. Alex was the cleverest person he knew but he had no idea what she was talking about.

"How many hours did your grandpa Mike say you'd have to practice if you wanted to become a professional soccer player?" she asked.

"10,000," said Jamie. It was one of the many pieces of advice Mike had given Jamie about soccer over the last year. Mike said that the top players only looked so good because they had practiced so long and from a very young age.

10,000 hours seemed like a huge amount but, for Jamie, every second he spent playing soccer was pure joy.

"Cool," said Alex, flicking the can into the air. "So let's get to the park and get practicing!"

And with that she volleyed the can all the way over to the other side of the street, where it looped perfectly into a nearby dumpster.

Jamie breathed a little more easily. He still felt hurt and worried by Pratley's comments but, at the same time, having Alex's support always helped.

Jamie was an electrifyingly quick left-winger and Alex was a brave, athletic goalkeeper. Together they made a pretty good pair, which was lucky because they both knew that, if they were going to stand any chance of beating the teachers and claiming that gleaming trophy at the end of the year, they would need to be part of the best students' team in the history of Wheatlands Primary School.

The Announcement

Wednesday, April 30th

"And now we move on to the details of the Teachers vs. 6th Graders Soccer Match," announced Mr. Karenza towards the end of the school assembly the next morning.

Jamie and Alex, who had been kicking each other playfully while Mr. Karenza was talking, suddenly stopped and sat up at their most alert.

"The match will take place on Thursday, the 17th of July, kicking off at 2:15pm," explained Mr. Karenza. "It should be a great way to end the school year, so remember to tell your parents and guardians to put the date in their diaries."

Jamie felt his stomach squirm. Parents. The word made him uncomfortable. The whole reason he was even at this school—why he was in the UK to begin with—was because of his dad.

His dad had been greedy, really greedy, and used his high-powered job to try to take other people's money. He had been caught and sent to jail. Jamie and his mom were left with no money and no place to live. That was why they left the States and came to the UK to be close to Jamie's grandfather, Mike. Jamie knew his mom just wanted to try and forget about everything and start again.

So, even though his dad would not be at the Teachers vs. Students match, at least he would have his mom and his grandfather there to cheer him on. Mike was Jamie's biggest fan and, although she knew nothing about soccer, Jamie's mom had promised to come and watch the game, too! She knew how incredibly important this match was to Jamie.

For a second, he allowed himself to imagine lifting the trophy and running over to show it to her. It would make her so proud.

"I'll referee the game as usual," continued Mr. Karenza, "and Mr. Pratley, who, as you know, remains unbeaten, will once again captain the teachers' team. Next week, we will hold a vote for the sixth graders to see who they want to be the students' captain."

Alex kicked Jamie in the shins and smiled at him. Everyone fully expected Jamie to be named captain of the students' side. He was the best player in the school and their greatest hope of ending the teachers' winning streak.

Jamie looked at Mr. Pratley, who was smirking confidently. Although Jamie and the other kids laughed at him when he lost his temper in class, they certainly did not laugh at him when it came to soccer. Pratley was a good player and he was ultra-competitive. Jamie remembered him celebrating last year's match as though he had just won the World Cup Final. This game was just as important to him as it was to the kids.

"Oh, and one final bit of news for you all," Mr. Karenza added, looking up and staring at the students in a way that made Jamie catch his breath. "Next week, we will be having a new boy joining sixth grade. It's late in the year for him to be doing so but there are special circumstances; the boy's father is coming from abroad to help design the new shopping mall in the center of Hawkstone. In any case, I hope you will all make him very welcome.

"In fact, I suspect he may very well have a big role to play in the soccer match, too, because the boy who is about join our school comes from the world capital of soccer... Brazil!"

Say It

Friday, May 2nd

"This guy Pratley is clearly just jealous of your talent, JJ," said Mike Johnson. "Forget him and what he said."

It was Friday evening and, because Jamie's mom, who was a nurse, had a double night-shift at the hospital, Jamie was staying at Mike's. It was good timing. Jamie had a few things on his mind, and Mike—Jamie called him by his first name rather than "Grandpa" because, these days, the pair were more like best friends than relatives—always seemed to give the best advice.

They were just finishing dinner – Mike's famous grilled cheese sandwiches, brimming with hot melted cheddar and provolone—and Jamie was beginning to open up about his problems at school.

Jamie shrugged. Pratley had made him feel stupid

for believing he was special, that he could make it as a professional. And despite what Mike had said, Jamie couldn't just forget it.

"Come on, JJ. Tell me," said Mike, wrapping his big, bear-like arm around Jamie. Sometimes Jamie wondered if he might be the strongest grandfather in the world. "What do you want from your life? Everyone wants something. What do you want?"

Jamie shook his head defiantly. Normally, he would have answered, quick as a flash: "To be a professional soccer player!"

However, now that he really thought about it and considered all the kids in the world who wanted to be pro soccer players compared to the number who actually made it, Jamie realized how high the odds were stacked against him. Statistically, no matter how much he practiced, there was probably as much chance of him winning the lottery as becoming a professional soccer player.

"Trust me," said Mike, smiling. "You've got something special, Jamie. I've known it from the very first time I ever saw you kick a soccer ball."

Jamie nodded. When it came to soccer, Mike knew what he was talking about. But Pratley's prediction wasn't the only problem.

"There's something else too," said Jamie. "There's a new kid coming to our school next week. He's Brazilian and everyone's really excited to see what he's like, how cool he's going to be, how great at soccer he's going— wait, but what if he's better than me? What if they make him captain of the students' team? What if he takes my spot in the team altogether?"

Mike shook his head. "Hang on a minute, JJ. I think you're looking at it the wrong way. How many hours have we spent talking about Brazilian soccer, watching those videos of their skills on the Internet, wondering where they got their touch of magic from?"

"A bunch," smiled Jamie. "More than Mom likes, anyway."

"And now you've got a Brazilian boy coming to your school? You shouldn't be worried, Jamie, you should be excited! If I were you, I'd be preparing a list of questions right now. If you want to be a professional, you should be asking this boy all the secrets of Brazilian soccer, and make sure you tell me!

"And, by the way," said Mike, suddenly getting quite excited, "if he's half as good as you, you two could develop a partnership and play upfront together for Hawkstone one day. What did you say his name was?"

"Rafael da Cruz," said Jamie.

"Yes," said Mike, warming further to the idea. "I like that. Johnson and da Cruz, the American and the Brazilian, the deadly striking duo to propel Hawkstone United to the league title..."

As Mike leaned back and conjured the image of his grandson inspiring his beloved Hawkstone United to lift the league title, Jamie shifted uneasily in his chair.

All of Mike's words had not yet convinced him that Pratley was wrong. And his hopes of captaining the students' soccer team were under grave threat too. He had learned that, in soccer, there was usually only room for one real star on any team. And Jamie knew that, just about now, flying across the sky, was a player from Brazil who might have the talent to outshine him completely.

Cruz Control

Monday, May 5th

"How many juggles can you do?" the boy demanded, arrogance oozing from every pore.

"I don't know," said Jamie. "Maybe 50 or 60…"

"Ha!" said the boy. "My record is 468."

Right there and then, in the school hallway, the boy started juggling the ball and before long, the whole school was watching and cheering.

"You're amazing! How do you do it?" all the kids asked, wowed by the boy's ability.

"Ha!" smiled the boy, flicking back his long black hair while continuing his kick-ups. "I have complete mastery of the soccer ball. I can even juggle the ball with my eyes shut—watch! My name is Rafael da Cruz. I am

Brazilian. This is what I do."

When he had finished showing off his tricks and skills, all the girls lined up to hug him. Alex even kissed him on the cheek and, while she did so, the boy just stared right at Jamie with a self-important smile.

"We are honored to have a Brazilian at our school!" said Mr. Karenza, joining the line to speak to the new transfer student.

"And I know the sixth graders have already decided that they would like you to be the captain in our big soccer match at the end of the year. Everyone has seen your skills. We all know you're a way better player than Jamie Johnson."

Jamie woke up in a dark mood. He could feel his anger spitting inside him like a volcano just before it is about to erupt.

He hardly slept all night and, when he had, his dreams had been filled with horrible visions of this boy from Brazil suddenly arriving at Wheatlands and snatching control of the whole school.

The thought of losing his position as the best player in the grade and perhaps even his friendship with Alex, too, made Jamie feel sick.

He tore into his breakfast sandwich and ground his teeth together as, without warning, his mind once again recalled the image of the cool Brazilian striding into school.

"I'll pick you up from Mike's at around 8:00pm tonight, got another double shif—" Jamie's mom was in the middle of saying as he slammed the front door shut behind him and stomped up the road to school.

Jamie already knew that this anger would be with him all day. His moods were like heavy coats, almost impossible to shake off. The truth was, he hated this Brazilian kid and he hadn't even met him.

At approximately 1:10pm that afternoon, a very strangely dressed boy walked into the Wheatlands cafeteria during lunch.

The boy was covered from head to toe in a huge beige waterproof jacket. The hood was over his head so far that his face was barely visible and the sleeves were stretched to cover his hands.

Without looking a single person in the eye or speaking to a soul, he sat down on a table all by himself and began to slowly eat a packed lunch.

All the children stared at him and a couple even introduced themselves and tried to start a conversation, but the boy still refused to say a word or make eye contact.

Fevered speculation began to mount. Was that him? Could it really be him?

None of the kids could believe it until, sure enough, just before the end of lunch, Mr. Karenza entered the cafeteria to make a short announcement.

"Everyone," he smiled, "this is Rafael da Cruz. Please make him feel very welcome."

7

Pratley's Plan

"Right, boys," said Mr. Pratley as the last of the lunch tables were removed from the cafeteria, which also served as the school's gymnasium. "We're going to play soccer today."

His announcement was met with complete and utter shock.

The boys and girls at Wheatlands were separated for gym. It made no sense to Jamie but he was starting to get used to it now.

This year, the girls got to go outside on the play-ground with the new teacher, Ms. Vetterlein, who allowed them to play soccer every week. Alex always raved about the quality of gym class. Not only was Ms. Vetterlein an awesome striker herself and an actual member of the Hawkstone United Women's Team, she also coached all the girls to become better players themselves. The only problem, Alex admitted, was that playing against Ms. Vetterlein in the Teachers vs. Students game was going to be an absolute nightmare!

Meanwhile, the boys had to be inside with Mr. Pratley, who had never let them play soccer even once. Yet today, for some reason, not only were they playing—but it was Pratley's suggestion.

Almost everyone cheered when he made his announcement.

The one person who did not cheer, however, was Jamie. There was something about this that he didn't like. Something that gave him a weird feeling. Why today? Jamie asked himself. Why is he letting us play soccer today?

"OK!" said Pratley with a worryingly large smile. "Johnson, you can be one captain and... let me see... yes, da Cruz... you can be the other."

"OOOOOOhhhh!" was the collective response from the rest of the players, who, as one, immediately understood the gravity of what was about to happen.

This was it! Already! Within just a couple of hours of Rafael da Cruz joining school, he was already going to be playing soccer against Jamie Johnson. A match-up between the best player in the school and the new kid from Brazil. People had been talking about this moment ever since they knew Rafael would be joining Wheat-

28

lands and now it was here.

And it was perfect timing too; all of this week, the sixth graders would be secretly voting for who their captain would be in the Teachers vs. Students game. This contest would undoubtedly show everyone who was the greatest soccer player in sixth grade.

For the first time, Jamie looked at the Brazilian boy properly. He took in his features: his short black curly hair, his dark, tanned skin. The contrast to Jamie's straight red hair and pale skin could not have been more obvious.

Glaring at his rival, Jamie felt his heart start to pump. A single bead of sweat began to trickle down his forehead. Then, as he watched Pratley pick the two teams, he felt a horror spread throughout him. The teams were wildly, outrageously unfair.

"What?" said Corey Snyder to Jamie, as both team line-ups were completed. "They've got Aaron ... and Dexter... and Kane... AND the Brazilian! That's way unfair! We're going to get CRUSHED!"

"Let's see what happens," responded Jamie. Outwardly, he was trying to appear calm. That was his responsibility as a captain. Inside, he was distraught. Now he understood exactly why Pratley was letting them play soccer; this whole game was designed to show Jamie up and make the Brazilian look great.

Pratley was trying to destroy Jamie's soccer reputation.

"Tackle Him!"

Jamie wished that Alex was with him. It was stupid that they split the boys and girls up for gym. If she was on Jamie's team now, he knew they could still win – even against the Brazilian.

It was as that thought crossed his mind that Jamie realized the Brazilian had been incredibly quiet during all of the pre-match commotion. Indeed, Jamie had not even heard the boy talk.

Jamie looked over and saw that, since Pratley told his students they were going to play soccer, the Brazilian boy had not moved an inch. He was still standing in exactly the same place: right in the middle of the gym, clutching on to what looked like some kind of notepad.

"Go on, da Cruz, get back into your own half,"

ordered Pratley. "We're going to kick off now. Perhaps you might demonstrate to Johnson that there is more to the game of soccer than just running fast!"

Pratley started laughing again. Jamie felt his anger rising.

Yet the boy remained exactly where he was. Was he in some kind of trance? Did he even understand English?

"Well come on then!" Pratley barked at the boy. "What are you waiting for?"

The boy frowned and shook his head.

"Get into your position!" yelled Pratley. "Let's see what you can do!"

And with that, Pratley blew his whistle and tossed the ball high into the air.

As the ball spiraled upwards, Jamie instantly felt the electricity shoot through his body. He felt the same powerful sensation when he started playing any game of soccer.

"It's called an adrenaline buzz," Mike had told him. "You get it if you're scared, angry or excited. It's your brain giving your body extra power to do what it needs to do."

Jamie knew his brain was right. It was time for him to do what he had to do.

"Yes, Corey!" called Jamie, immediately from the kick-off. "Go on, pass it!"

Jamie was already marked by Aaron Cody, one of the best players on the other side, but both Corey and

Jamie knew one thing: their team's best and only tactic was to get Jamie the ball as quickly as possible.

Kai chipped the ball to Jamie, who, feeling Aaron close behind him, turned him in one swift move...and now he was on the run.

Pushing the ball forward, Jamie raced like lightning down the gym, the other players fading away from him as he produced a run of breathtaking pace.

Within three seconds, Jamie's pure velocity took him from one end of the gym to the other and now, out of the corner of his eye, he registered that the biggest test was about to come. There was just one player left between him and the goalkeeper.

The Brazilian.

Jamie knew he had to get this absolutely right. He didn't have many tricks, so he would have to beat the Brazilian with his speed.

Jamie brought the ball to a complete stop to make sure the Brazilian was flat on his feet before speeding away from him again like a bullet.

Taking extra-special care to place his shot into the corner, Jamie swept the ball home to put his side up 1–0.

"Yes!" he roared, running to pick the ball out of the net before racing back to his own half, giving all of his jubilant teammates a high five on the way. He made sure to give the Brazilian and everyone else in the gym a stare. A stare that said the other side had some of the best players, but they didn't have Jamie.

As Jamie ran back past the Brazilian, he realized that the boy hadn't actually tried to tackle him when they were playing; he just let Jamie get through. Even now, he still had not really moved. For some strange reason, all the boy seemed to care about was holding on to that little notepad that he was carrying.

The game kicked off again straight away and immediately swung back the other way. Stung into action by Jamie's strike, Dexter and Kane Talbot, two skillful twins (one left footed, one right) combined to play a series of telepathic one-twos to rip right through the heart of Jamie's team. They even passed the ball to each other on the goal line before Dexter finished off the classic move to tie the game at 1–1.

Yet, even as their team was celebrating, Jamie noticed that the Brazilian was not involved in the action in any way. Instead, he opened his little notepad, took a pencil from his pocket, and began writing something down. In the middle of the game!

"Put that notepad away now!" shouted Pratley.

Hearing Pratley's yell, Rafael da Cruz reluctantly put the notepad back in his pocket. It was impossible not to notice that he had started to look very sad.

Jamie was utterly confused. Rafael was so different from the Brazilian boy that everyone had been expecting.

Perhaps, though, he was just a slow starter. Perhaps he needed to get used to his new surroundings before he felt comfortable enough to play. Or maybe he was being sneaky, fooling the other players by pretending that he was no good, getting ready to take everyone by surprise and stun them with his talent.

Jamie had to know the truth. He had to know how good this boy really was. There was only one way find out. Jamie had to take Rafael on again.

As soon as he received the ball, Jamie rampaged through the center of his opponents' defense. Again, he used no skills, just his raw, unmatchable pace. Almost inevitably, it resulted in the same situation: Jamie coming one on one with Rafael.

Let's see how you handle this one, he thought as he kicked the ball to one side of Rafael and scampered around the other to collect it. It was a simple but great move—one of Jamie's favorites.

Jamie was just sprinting past Rafael when the entire gym was suddenly filled with the tumultuous sound of pure anger.

"For God's sake... **tackle him!!!**" Pratley screamed. Stung into action by fear, Rafael turned and launched his body into Jamie's. The contact was immediate. Both players clattered into each other, tumbling over in a tangle of flying limbs. The screeching sound of skin burning on the gym floor told everyone that this was serious.

Jamie came to a halt and immediately looked at his bare arm. It was completely covered in a floor burn, and it hurt. A lot.

"What did you do that for?" Jamie snarled. "You knew I'd beaten you but you still took me down, you dirty cheat!"

"S-s-sorry," said Rafael, trying to get to his feet.

"So you should be!" shouted Jamie, converting all of his frustration into one powerful push to shove Rafael back down to the ground.

9

Thousands of Miles from Home

"Fighting in the gym! I can't tell you how disappointed I am by all of this. I really am," Mr. Karenza said gravely, leaning back in his chair, looking at the two offenders.

This was the first time in months that Jamie had been sent to the principal's office and he hated being here. Mr. Pratley could shout as loudly as he wanted and it never scared Jamie—if anything, he just found it funny. However, with Mr. Karenza it was the complete opposite: he had only lost his temper once in all the time Jamie had been at Wheatlands, but Jamie could still remember it vividly.

"Jamie, I would never have expected this of you," Mr. Karenza said. "You've been doing so much better and I thought, of all the Wheatlands' students, you would have been the one to make Rafael feel most welcome in our school.

"You know better than anyone how difficult it is to arrive in a new country and new school thousands of miles from your home. What do you think your mother would make of this if I told her?"

Jamie shook his head and looked at the floor.

"And Rafael, to get into a fight on your first day, within hours of arriving! After everything your father has done to get you into this school."

Mr. Karenza took off his glasses and rubbed his eyes. "And Mr. Pratley tells me that you pretty much refused to play soccer? Why was that, Rafael? Your dad told me you love soccer."

"I d-d-d-do love soccer," Rafael stammered.

Jamie stared at him. He realized it was the first time he heard Rafael say a whole sentence. Or rather, try to.

"B-b-b-b-ut I d-d-don't play. I l-l-love it in a d-d-d-different way."

As he attempted to speak, each letter and syllable was like a dagger in his throat. The more he tried to get the words out of his mouth, the harder and more painfully they seemed to stay blocked inside him.

Jamie was shocked, and he immediately understood why Rafael didn't want to speak earlier. He really felt for him.

"Fine," said Mr. Karenza, also a little more sensitively.

He was making notes on a piece of paper as he spoke.

"Well, we don't force anyone into anything here at Wheatlands so, in the future, you certainly don't have to play soccer if you don't want to. However, we cannot allow the fighting to go unpunished, so the two of you will help the lunch ladies clean up the cafeteria every day for the rest of the week, and if I ever hear about either of you fighting again, believe me, the consequences will be far, far worse. Is that clear?"

Both boys nodded and, as they did so, Jamie attempted to offer the smallest of smiles in Rafael's direction.

"What was all that about?" asked Alex as soon as Jamie and Rafael came out of Mr. Karenza's office.

"Fighting," Jamie said, watching Rafael walk away. "He's the one who started it, but I don't think it was really his fault."

"You and your temper," said Alex. "I feel sorry for whoever has to be your manager in the future."

But Jamie wasn't listening. He was watching Rafael slope away down the hallway by himself.

Looking at Rafael, it reminded Jamie of the way he felt when he had been in Rafael's position a year before. Back then, there was only one way to describe how Jamie felt and the same word described exactly how Rafael da Cruz had looked since the day he arrived at Wheatlands.

Lost.

Pollock's Delight

Friday, May 9th – four days later

Jamie stared at the baked beans splattered across the table. The red, gooey liquid was dripping off the edge and trickling down on to the bench below.

He took a deep breath, held his nose and wiped it clean.

Cleaning out the cafeteria after lunch was by far the worst punishment that the school handed out, and Jamie felt sure that Pratley had specifically requested it when he had sent the two boys to Mr. Karenza for their fight. Certainly, Pratley was watching them both with eagle eyes every day this week as they carried out their humiliating duties.

Yesterday, Pratley even came up to Jamie and said smugly, "Learning your lesson, Johnson?" as Jamie was emptying out the stinking trash can.

Still, at least now it was the end of the week and this would be the last day of the torture. Not that Jamie's plight was anything as bad as Rafael's; Jamie only had to clean up the mess. Rafael also had to put up with the teasing, and today it seemed to be getting even worse.

"Oh no, I've spilled my spaghetti on the floor!" said Edgar Pollock, the most annoying boy in fifth grade. He thought that just because his parents were rich (Jamie heard Edgar was kicked out of Stonecroft last year), he could order other people around. Worse still were the kids who hung around with him just because he had money.

"Will you come and p-p-p-pick it up for me, Rafael?"

Edgar and his friends erupted into raucous laughter and watched with delight as Rafael bent down and cleared up the mess. However, just as Rafael had finished, Pollock purposely tipped the rest of his plate over too.

"Oh no! Look what I've done now!" he cackled. "So sorry, R-R-R-Rafael!"

Jamie shook his head. Word was going around and some of the kids had started to talk about the fact that Rafael had a stutter. If someone had done to Jamie what Edgar had just done to Rafael, Jamie would have lost his cool and lashed out.

Yet as he watched Rafael slowly complete his dreadful, degrading mission, Jamie was struck by the fact that Rafael neither reacted nor showed he was affected.

There was no doubt that there was something very different about this boy. Jamie just couldn't determine whether that was a good thing or a bad thing.

Noted

"He's not what I was expecting—I know that for sure," said Jamie as he and Alex walked home, kicking a stone between them. "I think I like him but it's, you know, difficult to get close to him. And what's the thing with his notepad? Why's he always carrying it around?"

"Exactly," agreed Alex, flicking the stone into the air and volleying it further down the street to allow them to quicken their pace. "And that's not all. Have you seen him when we're playing soccer in the playground?"

Jamie shook his head.

"Just take a look on Monday," she smiled. "See what you think."

Saturday, May 10th

This was Jamie's favorite part.

Giving the usher his ticket, seeing them check it and then release the turnstile for Jamie to be able to push his way into the stadium. Into the home of Hawkstone United.

Mike gave Jamie season tickets for his birthday, just before the beginning of Hawkstone's latest campaign. It was the best gift Jamie had ever received! Even compared to all the cool stuff his dad used to buy him back in America.

He could easily have run up all 87 steps to get to their seats, but he knew that Mike couldn't run any more, so they climbed the steps together. It made Jamie sad to think Mike walked with a limp. And sadder still to think that the amazing career Mike would have had as a Hawkstone player was stolen away from him at such a young age by his horrific knee injury. But as they slowly climbed the stairs, Jamie felt proud and excited to be with a man who he admired so much. That was the point of being here at Hawkstone. It wasn't just the soccer. It was being together.

They always arrived half-an-hour before the kick-off in order to see all of Hawkstone's warm-up. Jamie loved watching the strikers pinging the balls into the top corner of the net from all types of outrageous angles. He could never understand why most of the fans stood outside the stadium eating and drinking right up until the last minute.

They were missing some of the best stuff. This was the chance to see how good these top players really were.

"Mike, can I ask you something?" said Jamie as the players jogged down the tunnel to receive their final instructions before the kick-off.

This was the last game of the season. Jamie and Mike had not missed a single home match all year. No matter how well or badly Hawkstone did, Jamie would support them for the rest of his life. From the first time that he walked into the stadium, Jamie knew Hawkstone was the club for him. They were part of who he was.

"Sure," said Mike, rising from his seat to stand up. He always did this just before the game started. It was his knee; if he sat down for too long without getting up, the knee locked and put him in excruciating pain.

"Was there ever any bullying when you went to school?" asked Jamie.

Mike's face changed and hardened.

"Is someone being mean to you about your dad again, JJ?" he demanded. "Tell me who it is and I'll take care of them. They'll be sorry they ever—"

"No, Mike, it's not me, don't worry," said Jamie. "It's someone else. That Brazilian kid I was telling you about before. He's arrived now and he's... kind of different.

Different from how we thought he was going to be, anyway, and some of the other kids, even the younger ones, are giving him a hard time."

"Oh," said Mike, straightening his coat and peering towards the tunnel. The players were beginning to assemble now. It was nearly time. "Well, you know that just because other kids are giving him a hard time doesn't mean that you have to."

Jamie nodded. But he also knew it wasn't as easy as that.

"I've never understood why people think being different is a bad thing," said Mike, putting his arm around Jamie's shoulder. Jamie knew that in a minute Mike would start the singing and the chanting. He once was the captain of the Hawkstone Youth Team. Now, he was the leader of the Hawkstone fans.

"Kids can be cruel," said Mike. "It comes from fear. They're scared of the other kids thinking they're not cool. What they don't understand is that real coolness is having the guts to go your own way—to be who you are.

"And anyway," he smiled. "Who wants to be exactly the same as everyone else? To me, that sounds seriously boring!"

Then Mike gave Jamie the nod. They both knew what it meant.

It was time to start shouting for Hawkstone at the very top of their lungs.

Get the Notepad

Monday, May 12th

"How long has he been there?" grinned Jamie.

It had been a good morning. No, it had been a great morning.

In the school assembly, Mr. Karenza announced that Jamie Johnson won the vote by what the principal described as a "very clear majority." Jamie was going to be captain of the Students' Team.

With the whole school watching, Jamie walked to the front, where he and Pratley, as the two captains, were told to shake hands and at least pretend they were best friends.

Jamie thought about tickling the inside of Pratley's palm as they shook hands but decided against it at the last minute. Always stand up for yourself, Mike told him, but never wind up your opponent—it only gives them an extra incentive to beat you.

"He's been there every second of every match we've played since he arrived," said Alex, answering Jamie's earlier question and snapping him back into the recess game they were playing.

Jamie looked to see that Rafael was crouching down behind one of the goals on the playground, almost entirely hidden by a car.

Squatting down like that, Rafael seemed as though he were on some kind of police stake-out or attempting to catch a glimpse of a leopard in the wild. He looked weird.

"Seriously?" said Jamie. "He's watched all our games at recess like that? And he's still writing in that note-pad! What is he putting in there?"

Jamie was intrigued. But there was no time to think about Rafael right now. There was a game going on and every day counted. Literally. Last night Jamie had calculated that there were only 43 more school days until the Teachers vs. Students game.

People were relying on him to make history. To be the first captain to lead the students to victory against the Teachers. It meant everything. He had to be focused on his game. He had to be ready.

"Yes!" Jamie shouted as Alex leapt high to snatch a

ball out of the air.

She looked up and saw that Jamie was tightly marked, but she also knew that she could still pass to him; he had the pace to get away. In a whir of motion, she spun the ball out to Jamie, who was waiting to collect it on the left wing.

Jamie stretched out his foot to accept the ball softly and bring it under his control. Use your feet like hands, Mike had told him once, as he showed Jamie how to kill the ball in an instant. He may not have been able to run any more, but Mike still had the touch of a professional.

As soon as the ball was with him, the soccer computer in Jamie's head kicked in. It calculated the distance between him and the goal and instantly worked out the rate at which he needed to run.

Then Jamie found his turbo gear, burning past two defenders in a flash. In his head, Jamie could hear the commentator shouting, ever more excitedly:

Johnson... still Johnson... still Johnson... STILL Johnson... He's going to SHOOT!

As Jamie drew back his left leg, everyone in the playground stopped to watch. The sun shone down from above the school building, illuminating the image of Jamie's body, perfectly shaped, ready to exert maximum power. Then Jamie brought his foot towards the ball with breathtaking speed.

He struck the ball so perfectly that it immediately

whistled through the air towards the goal. Jamie was just about to wheel away in celebration when he saw that his strike had actually not hit the net but instead had thundered into the angle of post and crossbar. It rebounded off the metal frame of the goal and was now ricocheting straight towards Rafael.

There was no time for Rafael to move. The ball was going far too fast.

"Ooooh!"

There was a gasp from everyone on the playground as the ball smashed brutally into the middle of Rafael's face, knocking him clean off his feet. As he fell backwards, hitting his head against the side of the car, his notepad went flying into the air.

"Get the notepad!" one of the kids shouted as they realized that this was their opportunity to grab the boy's most precious belonging. Hearing their plan, Rafael tried to scramble to his feet, but it was no use —he had hit his head so hard he barely knew where he was.

Jamie stood and watched. He saw the other boys charging towards Rafael, determined to steal his notepad. He saw Rafael, a tear nestled in his eye, desperately trying to stop them and something inside Jamie clicked.

It was almost the same feeling as when the anger washed over him...

Jamie had been teased before: for having red hair, for

being thin and small and pale, for being American. And the kids reserved the cruelest of taunts to make fun of Jamie's dad being in jail.

No, Jamie didn't feel anger towards Rafael. He wanted to help.

Jamie's eyes zoomed in on Rafael's location before scanning the area around him. Immediately, he detected where the notepad landed.

The other kids were all looking next to Rafael, but the notepad actually landed on the other side of the car, by the wheel. It must have looped up and over the vehicle when Rafael was thrown backwards by the power of Jamie's shot.

Jamie still had no idea what was so special about this notepad but he also knew that that didn't matter. It belonged to Rafael. That was what was important.

The computer in Jamie's head kicked back in, analyzing the distance he was from the notepad...but now the other kids had seen it too. It was a straight race between them and Jamie.

Jamie Johnson didn't lose races.

He dashed across the playground at Olympic speed and rolled under the car, scooping up the notepad just in time.

Then Jamie stood up as tall as he could and, with all the kids on the playground looking at him, he spoke with his loudest possible voice.

"Let's... just... give Rafael a break," he said, gasping for breath.

As the final word escaped from his mouth, Jamie realized how fast his heart was pumping. For a second, he just stood there panting.

Then he walked slowly over to Rafael and, resisting the temptation to look inside, handed the notepad back.

Rafael took the pad and held it to his chest, breathing what looked like a long sigh of relief.

"We're not all mean at this school," said Jamie, stretching out his hand to shake Rafael's. Rafael stared suspiciously at Jamie's outstretched hand as though he feared he was being lured into a trap.

"It's ok," smiled Jamie reassuringly. "I'm on your side. Friends?"

Then, for the first time, Rafael smiled back. A big, warm Brazilian smile.

"O-o-o-brigado, J-Jamie," said Rafael, shaking Jamie's right hand while clutching his notepad to his chest with the other.

Jamie looked at Rafael, slightly confused.

"Thank you?" he guessed.

Rafael nodded.

"Th-th-ank y-you."

"You Must Be a Genius!"
Friday, May 23rd – 11 days later

"Campiones, campiones olé, olé, olé!

Campiones, campiones olé, olé, olé!"

Hawkstone United, jointly managed by North American Jamie Johnson and South American Rafael da Cruz, were the Champions of Europe! With brave attack-minded tactics, they beat every other team on the continent. They were the kings of their favorite video game in the world, Soccer Manager!

"Shall we start a new one?" suggested Jamie as soon as they finished celebrating.

That was the thing about this game: the more they played, the more addicted they became.

"Load it up!" responded Rafael. "But this time I want us to try a new formation."

The seeds of the partnership had been sown in that moment when Jamie stood up for Rafael in the playground.

That day at lunch, Alex suggested that Rafael sit with her and Jamie and quickly he became a fixture alongside them in class too. Initially some of the other kids gave Jamie strange looks, as if to say, *Why are you being so nice to the weird kid?* But Jamie didn't care. He liked Rafael. And who wanted to be normal anyway?

Then, one day, in the middle of math class, when Pratley had his back turned, Rafael nudged Jamie playfully and tore a sheet out of his notepad, handing it to Jamie with a mischievous wink.

53

On the page was a drawing of Pratley with his eyes popping out and a booger coming from his nose, wagging his finger at Jamie, trying to discipline him. At the top was written "Pratley vs. Jamie", and at the bottom Rafael had written, "Is this right, Jamie?"

Jamie was overwhelmed by Rafael's artistic abilities and a bad case of the giggles. He was kicked out of class immediately, but he took the drawing with him.

Jamie didn't want Pratley to find out what he was laughing at and for Rafael to get into trouble too. Besides, he wanted to put that drawing up on his bedroom wall!

That incident seemed to make Rafael trust Jamie even more and when, the next afternoon, Jamie invited him back to his house for the first time, Rafael accepted.

They swiftly slipped into a comfortable routine: each day, after school, Jamie, Alex and Rafael walked to the park where Jamie took shots at Alex while Rafael looked on and made notes in his pad. Then they walked on to Alex's house and dropped her off at home before Jamie and Rafael would play Soccer Manager for hours and hours in Jamie's room, stopping only to go to the bathroom or to eat a snack. Their marathon sessions lasted until Rafael's dad, Bernard, came to pick him up in the evening. It worked perfectly for everyone because Bernard, who was an architect working on Hawkstone's brand-new shopping center, was always at the office until late anyway.

When Bernard arrived—generally in a suit and always looking serious but cool—Jamie and Rafael would simply pause the game and start it up again the next day.

Five days ago, while they were playing Soccer Manager, something quite amazing happened. During a snack break, Jamie asked Rafael to tell him again what soccer was really like in Brazil. He asked Rafael the same question every day.

Jamie was so fascinated by Brazilian soccer, he couldn't stop thinking about it. What he really wanted to know was what made the Brazilian soccer players so unique. What gave them that bit of magic and freedom in their play that no one else in the world seemed to possess?

Rafael was always happy to talk about Brazilian soccer, but what had been different about that day was the way in which he had answered the question, the way he had spoken.

"Soccer in Brazil is our life, our religion...it is everything," Rafael had smiled. "Every person in the country is in love with soccer. Me, for example. My dad took me to watch Palmeiras, his favorite team, when I was a baby! We go to watch them all the time and every game is like a party. The fans, they go to dance and sing. It is such a beautiful experience.

Oh, and by the way, Palmeiras have a new young player. He is an attacker called Arnaldo and he has the most amazing skills. He has the magic in his play that you are talking about. Believe me, everyone in the world will soon hear about him. "

It was only when Rafael paused for breath that they both stopped and looked at each other. Rafael did not stutter once the entire time he had been talking.

"Rafael! " Jamie beamed. "What just happened?! "

"I don't know..." grinned Rafael, exploring his new-found ability. "I spoke without a stutter... I still am! "

It continued for the whole afternoon and evening, but as soon as they were back at school, Rafael's stutter returned. And Rafael confided that it was still there when he was at home with his dad too. And yet these days, when it was just him and Jamie, chilling in Jamie's room, there was no sign of the stutter whatsoever. It was a kind of little miracle that neither of them talked too much about, just in case the stutter came back again.

"OK, we'll play as Palmeiras this time, and I want to try to play a 3-2-3-2 formation," said Rafael as Jamie loaded up a new game. They had been playing for four hours straight as Hawkstone United and already conquered Europe in the last game but they still wanted more. Now, as a Brazilian team, they wanted to take on the world!

The pair managing Palmeiras was also part of an important deal that the two boys had struck between them: Rafael agreed that, from now on, Hawkstone United would be his team to support in the Premier

League. In return, Jamie would now follow Palmeiras as his favorite Brazilian team. It meant exchanging lots of information about the clubs and players of the past and it also meant playing twice as many games on Soccer Manager to ensure that both Hawkstone and Palmeiras got their fair share of success.

But that was fine, especially as today had been Wheatlands' last day of school before spring break started! It couldn't have come any sooner. Jamie was ready to burst because he was used to taking a break from school far earlier in the year back in the States.

"Playing 3-2-3-2 is an experiment but I think it can work," Rafael explained, outlining his vision further. "We'll have three defenders at the back to deal with the one striker that most teams go with, a bank of two central defensive midfielders in front to keep track of the forward runs of the opposition midfield, three fast, creative central midfielders to cause problems between the lines, and two attackers—but not central ones. I want them to play out wide, to stop the opposing full-backs and, of course, also to cut in for lots of shots themselves. I want it to rain goals!"

Jamie did not respond. How could he? Just as his own brain could analyze and calculate speeds and angles on the soccer field, Rafael's seemed to be able to retain all of the information and tactics off the field. His powers of recall were phenomenal. It was as if he had a soccer version of a photographic memory.

"What do think?" smiled Rafael.

"I think you must be a genius!" said Jamie.

He was still staring at Rafael, in awe of his friend's vast soccer knowledge, when the doorbell rang.

Private Conversation

"You go and wait in the car, Rafa," said Bernard. "I want to speak to Jamie's mom for a minute."

Rafael looked at his dad and nodded. Then he gave Jamie a quick high five and a big smile.

"Go on," Bernard repeated. "I'll be there in five minutes."

"See y-y-ou s-o-on," said Rafael.

"Cool," said Jamie, realizing Rafael's stutter returned as soon as it wasn't just the two of them anymore. "Come over tomorrow so we can start another game with your new tactics."

Rafael didn't respond to Jamie's invitation. He simply smiled again—almost as though he knew something that Jamie didn't—and then left the house, closing the door behind him.

For a second, there was silence, both Jamie and his mom staring at Bernard, wondering what he wanted.

"Would it be OK if I spoke to your mom alone for a bit?" Bernard asked. He looked so serious, Jamie wondered if something really bad had happened, but that was how Rafael's dad always looked: cool but definitely serious.

Jamie walked up the stairs, opened the door to his bedroom and then shut it loudly, but he didn't go inside. The noise was just to make sure that Bernard and his mom thought he was in his room. There was no way he was going to miss this.

Jamie crouched down and, very slowly, so as not to make even the tiniest creak in the floorboards, crawled to the top of the stairs, where he would be able to hear what they were saying without them being able to see him.

"....I know it would make Rafael extremely happy and me too," Bernard was saying. Jamie could hear the kettle boiling. His mom always made tea when she talked to people in the kitchen.

"Milk? Sugar?" she asked.

"No, just black is great, thank you," said Bernard. "So, what do you think, Karen? We think Jamie would love Brazil and it would be our absolute pleasure to have him with us."

Jamie's whole body froze. Did he just hear what he thought he heard?

"There you go," she said, her voice completely calm. "Listen, Bernard, it really is very kind of you to make such an offer and I'm sure Jamie would absolutely love to go to Rio with you but... well, there's no way we can accept, I'm afraid."

"I see..." said Bernard.

At the top of the stairs, Jamie was beginning to shake. This was too big, surely she couldn't be saying no. *Why?* he silently mouthed in anguish.

"And why is that?" asked Bernard.

"Where do I start?" said his mom. "Jamie's only just getting himself settled in the UK now. To uproot him again, it's the wrong time. And Brazil is the other side of the world!

"The longest he's ever spent away from home is two nights on a school trip, now suddenly we're talking about a whole week, not to mention the fact that there's absolutely no way on earth that we can afford it."

Jamie clenched his fist and bit it as hard as he could. Going to Brazil would be, without doubt, the most exciting thing he could do in his life—even more than going back to America—and yet his mom was saying there was "no way on earth" it was going to happen. All he wanted to do was scream.

"Maybe if you could wait until the summer vacation, then the boys will know each other a bit better and we'll all have time to prepare for it rather than just...

springing it on us the night before."

"I do realize this is last minute," acknowledged Bernard. "It's just that Rafael and I have to go back this week—we fly in the morning. There is something we have to be there for that can't be changed.

"We only had the idea last night. Rafael was telling me how much he likes Jamie and how kind Jamie has been to him and we just thought it would be a nice idea, make it a really nice spring break for him. We are sure Jamie would love Brazil.

"And, please," he continued, "don't worry about the cost. It would be my pleasure to pay for Jamie's ticket. It's the least I can do. So just let me know if you change your mind."

Help

Jamie waited until he heard Bernard's BMW start up and drive off. Then he sprinted down the stairs and unleashed his venom.

"Why did you do that?!" he screamed at his mom. His face was bright red with fury.

"Jamie! You were listening? You shouldn't have been listen—"

"Do you have any idea how much this would mean to me? For anyone who loves soccer, Brazil is the one place in the world you dream of going. I'll never get a chance like this again in my life and you're ruining it! Do you want me to hate you?!"

"Jamie! Do NOT talk to me like that! I'm not doing this to be cruel to you. I'm trying to do what's right. It's all way too quick to make such a big decision."

Jamie had already slammed the door behind him. He was running. Sprinting as hard as he could, hammering out the frustration and anger through his legs on to the pavement. He was tearing through the streets, his body charged with rage.

If he could, he would have ran all the way to America and begged his dad to help him, but he knew that wasn't possible. There was only one place left to run.

"You should never say you hate anyone, JJ. Least of all your mom," said Mike, once Jamie had got it all out. For the first few minutes after he arrived Jamie had been so upset he wasn't even been able to talk.

"You need to apologize," said Mike, walking into the kitchen. "I'm up for a grilled cheese. You?"

"No way!" snapped Jamie, ignoring Mike's offer. "Why should *I* apologize? She should be the one saying sorry to me! She's the one stopping me from doing the most amazing thing I'm ever going to do in my life! What's wrong with her?"

Jamie's whole body was a cauldron of boiling resentment. Why didn't she just concentrate on her own life instead of ruining his?

"She's not some cruel dictator," said Mike, slipping a bit of cheese into his mouth as he prepared his sandwich. "She's your mom."

Jamie got up and angrily kicked Mike's tennis ball

against the wall. He couldn't sit still.

"Just do something, Mike," said Jamie, trying to hit the ball again, even harder this time. But he swung his foot at the ball so violently he missed it altogether. This wasn't the first time this had happened; when he argued with his mom, his soccer skills always seemed to suffer, which only made him more frustrated.

"Make her understand what this means. This is Brazil! Aren't you the one who said I should be asking Rafael everything about soccer over there? Well, this is my chance to actually go. Every day will be like the best soccer lesson ever! Don't you always tell me never to give up on my dreams? This is my dream! You know that! You've got to stop her, Mike! Please!! Before it's too late!"

Mike took a firm grip of his grandson and held him in a cool stare.

"Jamie," he said, with a strong, even voice. "Everything that you have in this world, including your existence, is because of that woman. Remember that. Now, do you want my help or not?"

Language of Soccer

Jamie and his mom had both been going crazy, for different reasons. His mom knew she couldn't be late for her shift at the hospital for the second time this week and Jamie was beyond desperate to know what Mike and Bernard had been talking about for this long.

Once Jamie calmed down (having eaten two of Mike's jumbo-sized grilled cheese sandwiches) Mike had taken Jamie home and Jamie apologized to his mom for losing his temper. Then Mike had suggested that perhaps he should just go and have a chat with Bernard, if only to get a bit more information. What harm could it do?

Jamie gave Mike the address and Mike immediately took off. But that was two-and-a-half hours ago. Since then, they heard nothing.

When Karen and Jamie finally spotted Mike walking back up the street, they could both tell from the look on his face that something was up. He was in a world of his own. He even stopped to sit on a bench outside for a couple of minutes, looking up at the sky.

"Sit down," he said to both of them when he finally came in. "There's quite a lot to tell you."

Mike looked at Jamie for a second with such kind eyes that it made Jamie feel warm inside. Then his grandpa started to speak.

"Rafael's mom died two years ago," he began. "Her name was Stephania and she had been sick for a very long time. It must have been awful for them all, and since the day that she passed away, that exact day, Rafael has suffered from the most terrible stutter.

"They can't find a cure. The doctors have told Bernard that the only way Rafael will get over it is by feeling comfortable and happy again. That's the reason that Bernard brought Rafael over here: to give him a change of surroundings, to try to make him happy again. And to maybe find one person who Rafael can trust. And it seems that that person is Jamie.

"JJ, you never told us that Rafael doesn't stutter when it's just you and him."

Jamie nodded.

"Anyway, this is exactly what Bernard was hoping for.

He called the doctors this morning and they told him that it made sense. That trust and friendship and feeling comfortable are all elements that would help Rafael find his voice again.

"Bernard believes that it's about the soccer too. He's got this theory that when Jamie and Rafael are talking about soccer, they are speaking in another language. He believes Rafael doesn't stutter when he's speaking the language of soccer."

Jamie nodded. Rafael was fluent in soccer all right.

"The last thing Bernard wants to do is split the boys up right now but he says that he and Rafael have to go back to Brazil for spring break. There is an event they both need to attend. It's been planned for a long time.

"That's why he would like Jamie to go with them. Not only would he and Rafael get to spend more time together but, it would also be a kind of thank you to Jamie."

Mike paused.

"It was so difficult hearing him talk, Karen. The man looked like he has not smiled for such a long time."

When Mike had finished speaking, there was complete silence in the room.

"Well, I can see why you were over there for such a long time," said Jamie's mom, kissing Jamie on the forehead almost without noticing. "I had no idea what Rafael had been through. And if Bernard thinks that

Jamie being there will help Rafael speak fluently again, then I understand a bit better why he's so keen for Jamie to go... but it all puts a lot of pressure on Jamie, doesn't it?"

"Bernard's not expecting anything," said Mike. "He doesn't see Jamie being there as some kind of magic cure for Rafael's stutter. He just doesn't want to split the boys up at the moment. He thinks they are good for each other, so he's inviting Jamie to come along, enjoy Brazil and see what happens. He says he even knows a great coach that can teach Jamie all the Brazilian soccer skills."

Jamie squirmed with excitement. Ever since Pratley told him he wouldn't make it as a professional, he had been really depressed about his chances of fulfilling his dream. But if he could go to Brazil, if he could learn their skills, be trained in their magic, surely that would give him the extra edge so that one day he really could turn his dream into reality.

He didn't say anything. Instead, he just stared pleadingly into his mom's eyes. He had to make her understand how much he wanted this opportunity.

"I'm just... very worried about this," said Karen. "It's so soon and, if they're going first thing in the morning, that means Jamie would have to fly by himself tomorrow night. I don't know. I just don't know..."

Mike looked at Jamie and then he looked at Karen. His eyes seemed to sadden a little.

"Do you remember how I reacted when you had your accident?" he asked.

Karen nodded. Jamie could sense her body tighten.

Jamie knew that, when she was a kid growing up in the UK, his mom had been good at riding horses. Seriously good. She had been one of the best in the whole country but then, when she was fifteen, she had a really bad fall and broke her back. Jamie knew she still kept all of her medals because he had seen them in a special box under her bed.

"I told you that you weren't ever allowed to ride again after that day, didn't I?" Mike said.

"And I... hated you for it," replied Karen. "But you were right. If I fell again, anything could have happened. I could have been paralyzed."

Mike shook his head. "Once you recovered, there was no greater risk of you falling and hurting yourself than any other rider," he said. "I just didn't want you to ride because I was scared."

Mike was twisting the ring on his finger as he spoke. Jamie could tell he was choosing his words very carefully.

"I should have listened," Mike said. "I should have understood what my child wanted from life, what her biggest dream was, and supported her every step of the way. I didn't do that for you, Karen, and I'm so sorry."

Jamie's mom started to cry, which immediately made

Jamie cry too. Seeing his mom upset cut all the way through him.

"Don't be sad, Mom," Jamie said, giving her the biggest bear hug he could manage. For the first time, he realized that he got some of his sporting talent from her. "Why don't you start riding again now?"

Karen shook her head, wiped away her tears and attempted to smile.

"I just think that, if he doesn't go, Jamie will always be wondering what it would have been like," said Mike. "And believe me, life is not about wondering, it's about doing."

Karen blew her nose. She still looked unsure.

"Your boy has a dream, love," Mike said softly, smiling at Karen. "And this trip to Brazil can help him achieve it. What do you say?"

Not the World's Greatest Dancer

Saturday, May 24th

"Just do me one favor, JJ," said Mike, looking at Jamie through the rear-view mirror. Mike, Jamie and Karen had been on the drive to the airport for two hours now.

"Make sure you take in every second of what you are about to experience. To fly to Brazil as an 11-year-old boy...it's incredible. Nothing like this will ever happen to you again."

Jamie nodded. He knew.

"JJ, did I ever tell you that one of my ambitions in life was to go to Brazil, watch a match out there and then dance in the streets all night, you know, proper samba style?"

Jamie and Karen couldn't help but chuckle. Mike was good at many things, but he was far from the world's greatest dancer.

"Just to do something spontaneous like that," Mike said. "That's what makes you feel alive."

"What does spontaneous mean?" asked Jamie.

"Doing something on impulse," replied Mike. "Forgetting the risks and all the reasons not to do something and just doing it anyway."

Jamie nodded. He understood. That's what the best soccer players did. They took a risk. They produced a skill from nowhere just at the right time.

"I haven't been spontaneous enough in my life," said Mike. "It won't happen for me now. So take it all in, JJ. Never forget how lucky you are to be able to live out a dream."

Watching Mike as he drove steadily on towards the airport, Jamie felt a familiar mixture of sadness and happiness settle upon him.

When does it become too late to make your dreams come true? he wondered.

Thε Book

Jamie sat down in his seat, opened his backpack and took out the two items Mike had given him seconds before he got on the plane.

The first was a brand new phone—Jamie's first ever—so that they could stay in touch at any time.

The second was a small booklet that Mike stayed up all night writing for Jamie.

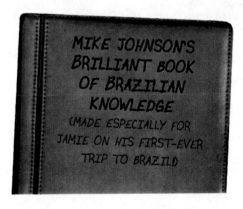

MIKE JOHNSON'S
BRILLIANT BOOK
OF BRAZILIAN
KNOWLEDGE
(MADE ESPECIALLY FOR
JAMIE ON HIS FIRST-EVER
TRIP TO BRAZIL)

THE HISTORY OF
SOCCER IN BRAZIL!

Right, JJ. The story of Brazilian soccer, so the legend goes, begins way back in 1894 when a British boy named Charles Miller arrived in the Brazilian port of Santos! Miller was in Brazil to visit his father and had just spent time at boarding school, where he had been honing his skills at his favourite sport (guess what that was?).

He stepped off the boat with two soccer balls. I guess those two balls changed the history not only of Brazil but also of the whole game of soccer.

Apparently they have a saying in Brazil:
"Os ingleses o inventaram, os brasileiros o aperfeiçoaram."
"The English invented it, the Brazilians perfected it."

IMPORTANT FACTS ABOUT BRAZIL!!

- There is no such language as Brazilian. A lot of people think that they speak Spanish in Brazil. They are wrong! In Brazil, they actually speak a Brazilian form of Portuguese. This is because Portuguese people settled there from as early as the sixteenth century.

- Although it will be hot for you, this is not the Brazilian summer. Their summer is Jan/Feb time. Weird, eh? Imagine Christmas on the beach!

- Brazil is a huge country. And when I say that I mean MASSIVE. Both in terms of size and population, it is the fifth largest country in the world. It's nearly the same size as the whole of Europe!

- The Amazon River flows through Brazil. It is the second longest river in the world. Do you know what the longest is, JJ? (It begins with the letter "N".)

- Brazilians love nicknames, especially for their footballers! Pelé's real name is Edson Arantes do Nascimento. But Pelé just works so much better!

- In Brazil there is the most unbelievable nature. Not only are there all the beaches, but there's also the jungle! Jaguars and pumas (both big hunting cats) live there. So do poisonous frogs, massive snakes and ... piranhas. Remember I told you about them, JJ? They are the fish that have sharp teeth — they sometimes attack humans!

(Don't worry, they're in the Amazon River, which is nowhere near where you are in Rio - PHEW!)

OK, that's enough of the science bit! Now for some **soccer** facts!

- Brazil is the only country to have played in every World Cup there has ever been!

- They play **soccer** everywhere. Even in the swamplands of the Amazon!

- These are the biggest clubs in Brazil and the cities in which they play.

Club	City
Vitória	Salvador
Goiás	Goiânia
Atlético Mineiro	Belo Horizonte
Atlético Paranaense	Curitiba
Avaí	Florianópolis
Bahia	Salvador
Botafogo	Rio de Janeiro
Ceará	Fortaleza
Corinthians	São Paulo
Coritiba	Curitiba
Cruzeiro	Belo Horizonte
Figueirense	Florianópolis
Flamengo	Rio de Janeiro
Fluminense	Rio de Janeiro
Grêmio	Porto Alegre
Internacional	Porto Alegre

Palmeiras	São Paulo
Santos	Santos
São Paulo	São Paulo
Vasco da Gama	Rio de Janeiro

- On the beach, Footvolley is the most popular game. It's the same as volleyball but you use your feet, not your hands!

- Futsal is also seriously popular. This is indoor soccer but with smaller goals and a smaller ball. It makes you concentrate more on skill. You know Ronaldinho grew up playing futsal – see what I mean about it improving your skills!

- Listen out for the word **caneta** when you're over there. That's what the Brazilians call a nutmeg – when you kick the ball between someone's legs. They go crazy for it over there, apparently!

Ok, let's slip in a little math for you here, JJ - to keep your brain alive while you're on vacation!

Pelé scored 77 goals in 92 games for Brazil. He scored 12 goals in 14 games at the World Cup. Which is the better ratio?

Ha! I can hear your head spinning from here! You see, JJ, I'll keep working you even in your spring break! And you know why? Because, if you want to be a great soccer player, that mind of yours is going to be as important as those feet!

This was by far the best book Jamie ever read! The more facts that he could get about soccer the better! And there was still another whole chapter on the legends of Brazilian soccer to go. The revving of the engines told Jamie that the plane was ready to take off.

He put the booklet down and looked out of the window.

He thought that his mom and Mike would probably be nearly home by now. Jamie knew how difficult his mom found it to let him go on this trip. That was why, just before he got on the plane, he turned and ran back to give her one more hug.

"Thank you, Mom," he'd said. "Thank you so much for letting me go for my dream."

The engines revved once more and the airplane sped down the runway.

Jamie's journey was about to begin.

PART TWO

The Beach

Sunday, May 25th

"Are you sure you want to wear that shirt to the beach?" asked Bernard. "It'll be hot."

Jamie took a big spoonful of cereal and nodded.

At 1:00pm, this was a very late breakfast but, then again, Jamie had only gone to sleep at four in the morning. Rafael and Bernard had picked Jamie up from the airport and driven him back to their home.

As soon as they turned into the driveway, Jamie was impressed. They must have owned one of the nicest houses in Rio de Janeiro. Apparently it was only a ten-minute walk to the beach, which was lucky because that was exactly where he and Rafael were heading straight after breakfast.

Jamie texted his mom to say he arrived safely just before he went to sleep. He spent the whole night dreaming about playing soccer on the beach!

Both Rafael and Bernard had promised Jamie that there was someone special he would meet today. Someone who could help him learn how to play soccer Brazilian style...

"I have to wear this shirt!" Jamie smiled, answering Bernard. He looked down at his black and white Hawkstone United shirt. He had been given it by the club on the day he had been a Junior Captain for them. "It gives me good luck and helps me to play better. You might not understand. It's a superstitious kind of thing."

Bernard and Rafael raised their eyebrows at each other.

"What?" asked Jamie. "Why are you looking at each other like that? Lots of soccer players are superstitious."

"I know that," said Bernard. He looked serious, but then again he always looked serious. "But to say to a Brazilian soccer fan that they don't understand superstition is like saying to an Eskimo he doesn't understand snow. Isn't that right, Rafael?"

Rafael nodded proudly. "O-one h-h-hundred p-p-per cent."

"Perhaps you should tell Jamie about the dog that had to pee," Bernard suggested to his son, who immediately cracked up laughing. "If he thinks he's superstitious, wait until he hears about Biriba!"

"Botafogo is a very famous team in this country from here in Rio," began Rafael, without a hint of a stammer as they left the house to head to the beach. It was amazing: as soon as it was just the two of them, Rafael's speech was completely uninhibited. Jamie wished Bernard could see it. He even wondered whether he should record Rafael speaking like this and play it to Bernard. That would be too risky, though; if Rafael found out, he wouldn't trust Jamie any more and, from what Jamie understood, trust was the whole reason that Rafael felt able to speak freely with Jamie in the first place.

Bernard was right. It was boiling. Jamie could feel the sweat trickling down his forehead instantly. He looked up at the sun and the golden rays shining down on him dazzled his eyes. He looked around at the busy streets, all hustle and bustle—people cleaning the cars, dusting off mats and talking.

At home in the UK, most people ignored each other in the street but here, just like where Jamie had grown up in Maine, everyone seemed to be friendly and saying hello to each other. The chatter of conversation seemed to be coming from everywhere. And so did the colors —everyone seemed to be wearing bright, vibrantly colored clothes.

"...and perhaps Botafogo might be the most superstitious team in Brazil," Rafael said, continuing his story with a sly smile that promised something entertaining to come. "I am going to tell you a true story of something that happened in the 1950s.

"So, imagine this: the reserve team of Botafogo were playing a game and they were on the attack. The striker was through; one on one with the goalkeeper. He looked up and took a shot and, at that precise moment, a mongrel of a dog came running on to the field after the ball. It ran straight at the keeper and completely distracted him because he didn't know whether to look at the ball or the dog! So the ball went in the net and the referee allowed it! Goal to Botafogo! Or gooooool! as we say here!"

"No way!" said Jamie. "Assist to the dog!"

"You got it! The dog helped them take the lead!!" joked Rafael.

They were turning off the main road now and into some smaller side streets. There was a steep downward hill that offered, in the near distance, a view of the shimmering blue sea. Jamie took in a breath. He had never seen anything quite so beautiful.

"Anyway," Jamie said, suddenly coming back to Rafael's story. "I thought this was supposed to be a story about superstition?"

"Jamie!" said Rafael. "I haven't even got to that part yet!"

"Well, get on with it!" Jamie laughed. "We'll be at the beach in a minute and then I'll be too busy playing to talk!"

"It turns out that the dog was a stray," said Rafael. "And, because it helped to score a goal, one of the Botafogo players adopted it and it became the mascot of the club, coming to every game. They called it Biriba.

"And you know what they did? If they were ever doing badly in a game and needed a break, they would let Biriba run on to the pitch and scamper all over the place until the referee stopped the game.

"The Botafogo players never helped to get Biriba under control, so it always took ages, and by the time the match got restarted, Botafogo reorganized and were ready to make a comeback. It was such a good plan and the dog became so famous that other teams even threatened to kidnap Biriba. Or do you say dog-nap him?"

"I don't know!" laughed Jamie. "Fair enough, Rafa, that is a pretty good story."

Rafael grabbed Jamie's hand so hard that they both stopped walking. Rafael was shaking his head and his face was going red with laughter.

"That's not even the best part!" he giggled. "One day before a really big match, all the players were in the locker room, warming up, you know, talking tactics, making their plans for the game when, out of nowhere, Biriba, you know... did his... pee on the full-back's leg! Right there in the dressing room."

"No way!" said Jamie. "That's gross!"

"Anyway, so Botafogo end up winning the game.

And the president of the club, the man in charge of the whole of Botafogo, gets to hear about what happened—that before the game Biriba had peed on the full-back's leg. Well, this president was so superstitious that, from that day on, he made it an actual order that BEFORE EVERY SINGLE GAME Biriba had to pee on the same defender's leg because it gave them good luck!"

The two boys had to stop. They were laughing too much.

"What? Every game the same player had to get peed on?!" said Jamie, in between his convulsions. "How do you even know this stuff? Imagine if that happened in the Premier League!"

"I know! I know!" said Rafael. "And to top it off, that year Botafogo won the league!! And everybody believed it was down to the peeing dog! You see—we know about being superstitious in Brazil!"

The Streets

The boys' laughter had only just subsided when they turned the corner and entered another set of streets.

Instinctively, Jamie understood that they had turned a corner in more than one way. He looked at Rafael, who was already staring at him.

"These are the poor streets," said Rafael. "This is what we call a *favela*."

Jamie looked around him. They had been walking for less than five minutes from the luxurious area in which Rafael lived and yet, suddenly, they reached a different world. Poverty seemed to drift through these streets like smoke in the air.

However, there, right in the middle of it all, looking as happy as anyone Jamie had ever seen in his life, were seven or eight kids, dashing around playing soccer.

The scene hypnotized Jamie. The kids—boys and girls of all different skin colors—were running barefoot along the gravel street, chasing after a ball, which was clearly badly punctured. Their clothes were ripped, their faces and hair were very dirty and yet they seemed to be having so much fun. The soccer they were playing was full of joy.

Suddenly, one of the kids kicked the ball in the direction of Jamie and Rafael and now all of the players were rampaging towards them. Without thinking, Jamie advanced towards the ball at the same time as the smallest and thinnest of the kids.

The little Brazilian boy, who was wearing a ripped and tattered old Brazil soccer shirt, got to the ball just before Jamie and knocked it right between Jamie's legs, gleefully shouting: "*Caneta! Caneta!!*"

Within seconds, all of the other kids were crowding around Jamie, laughing, pointing at his red hair and grabbing at his Hawkstone jersey.

And now, holding the punctured ball under his arm, the boy who just did the caneta returned too. He also started grabbing at Jamie's Hawkstone shirt. He seemed to want to take it from Jamie.

Jamie's body tensed. He would never allow anyone to take this shirt. Every part of him was ready to fight.

But Rafael put his arm around Jamie and walked him away from the group, waving back at the other kids as he did so.

"They are just interested in you because you are different," said Rafael. "You don't have to be scared of them."

"I wasn't scared!" replied Jamie, a little too eagerly.

"Good," said Rafael. "Because I wanted to show you these streets. Many people, they come to Rio and all they see—all they want to see—is the beach. But Rio is about the streets as much as it is about the beach. Only when you understand that do you start to understand our city. Oh, and by the way, *caneta* means n—"

"Nutmeg—I know," said Jamie, feeling a twinge of embarrassment at having the ball knocked through his legs by a little kid.

"Those kids can play," he acknowledged. "They have talent."

"Of course they have talent!" laughed Rafael. "They are Brazilian."

The Master

"What's wrong with here?" asked Jamie.

It seemed as good a spot as any. There was space on the beach and people playing soccer all around.

"No, we are not there yet," said Rafael, trekking ahead, further along the beach.

Jamie and Rafael had been walking along the beach for 15 minutes but it felt like six hours. Jamie could feel his skin roasting in the scorching sun and his throat was so dry he would have given his life's savings to have just one glass of ice-cold water.

And all of this was to find some man. This mysterious person who was somehow going to help Jamie play soccer Brazilian style.

Jamie watched Rafael march on. He had no choice but to follow.

"Whoever this guy is, he better be worth it," Jamie muttered to himself.

"There!" said Rafael a few minutes later. "There he is! *Olá, Mestre!*"

He was shouting and waving to someone by the sea.

Jamie followed the line of Rafael's wave. He looked past the string of cafés with music blaring out, beyond the sunbathers strewn across the beach and on towards a group of kids near the sea.

Even from his vantage point, Jamie could see that all of the kids were practicing their skills. They were displaying acrobatic ability, continuous concentration and sublime skill. And every single one of them was beaming with pleasure. This was something close to soccer heaven.

Standing next to the soccer players, watching their every move, stood a tall man with his arms folded. He had clearly heard Rafael's shouts but had not reacted in any way.

Then, after another minute, he said something to one of the players and began walking towards Rafael and Jamie.

Jamie could sense just by Rafael's reaction that this was a significant person. He strained his eyes to get a closer look at the approaching man.

There was something in the way that he moved along

the sand of the beach so smoothly that reminded Jamie of a lion prowling its territory. His natural movements spoke of power, athleticism and strength. And yet, as he drew nearer still, Jamie recognized that this was not a young man, perhaps about 60-years-old. About the same age as Mike.

The man had a mane of long, thick greying black hair, which contrasted with the short, clipped beard that framed his lean, chiseled facial features. His skin was brown and creased from years in the sun but his green eyes seemed bright and inquisitive.

As the man drew within a few feet of the pair, Rafael looked at Jamie and smiled.

"Jamie," he said proudly. "Get ready to meet *O Mestre*—The Master."

"Your Feet Must Be Free"

"M-M-Mestre, th-th-is is J-J-Jamie," Rafael had said. "He wants to l-l-learn."

Mestre had smiled kindly at Rafael and gestured for the boys to follow him to the area by the sea where all the skills were being demonstrated.

Now, as he walked behind Mestre and Rafael, who seemed to know each other pretty well, Jamie could feel his feet starting to tingle. They wanted to do just one thing: kick a ball.

As soon as they arrived in the area where the other kids were practicing their skills, Rafael sat down cross-legged in the sand, got his notepad out of his bag and began writing immediately.

Meanwhile, Jamie watched the boy next to him flick the ball into the air, trap it on the back of his neck, flick it back into the air and then bicycle kick it into the sea! Then he dove in and swam with incredible speed to recover it. The boy seemed to be a mixture between Tarzan and a freestyle soccer-skills sensation!

Then Jamie looked at the girl next to him. She was balancing the ball on top of her head, walking down towards the sea and then back up the beach. She seemed so in control of her body. As she walked, her eyes were fixed firmly on the ball on her forehead and a smile was fixed firmly on her face.

These were just two of around 40 kids all practicing, demonstrating and perfecting different ball skills, a few of which Jamie saw before on the Internet but most of which were completely new to him.

Jamie shook his head at Rafael in delighted disbelief. This set-up—being part of this Brazilian school of skill on the beach—was even more than he had been hoping for! Rafael simply looked up from his notepad, smiled and gave Jamie a big thumbs up in return.

Looking around him, Jamie quickly came to a conclusion: he could not spend much time amongst such skillful players without becoming at least a little more skillful himself.

And now Mestre turned his attention to Jamie. The man's green eyes reflected the deep, mysterious color of the sea.

"Shall I go and get one of those balls?" Jamie asked, beaming from ear to ear.

Mestre shook his head. He was pointing to Jamie's sneakers.

"Your feet," said Mestre, speaking English with an incredibly thick Brazilian accent. "This is where it all begins. They must be free. You must touch the ball with your feet. Listen to the word: FOOTball. It starts with the foot."

Jamie understood about 50 percent of what Mestre was saying. He grasped enough, though, to work out that he should take off his sneakers. However, within seconds of putting his feet down on the sand, the heat was scorching them.

"Oweeee!" he screamed, hopping from foot to foot. The other kids turned to look at Jamie and laughed. With his strange, jerky, jumping movements, he looked as though he was doing some kind of funky dance.

"Use the sea to cool your feet," advised Mestre. "And then run to the café over there and ask them for my water."

The "café over there" was about half a mile away. By the time Jamie got back with Mestre's bottle of water, his face was the same color as his hair—bright red—and his legs were drained of all their energy. Jamie had run plenty on the beaches in Maine when he was younger but, somehow, the sand in Brazil felt different and more tiring than any other surface on which Jamie had run on before.

However, there was another even greater problem.

"The soles of my feet are completely burnt!" Jamie complained. "I just tried to kick a ball and it was agony! How long will it take to heal?"

His question seemed to evoke a half-smile from Mestre.

"You will play in a few days," he said.

"A few days?!" Jamie shouted in high-pitched anguish.

He was so confused. Mike always encouraged him to play and train as often as possible, while this man, this master, seemed to be stopping him from playing.

"That's crazy!" Jamie snapped. "I need to play now!"

But Jamie's words seemed to have no impact on Mestre. They were like tiny grains of sand hitting a huge rock.

"You will play when you are ready. Only when you are ready," Mestre replied before turning away to focus on all his other students.

The Photo

"You have to trust him, Jamie," said Bernard. "He knows what he is talking about."

They had just finished dinner and Jamie told Bernard that the only thing his feet managed to do during a whole day at the beach was get burned.

"You know, Jamie," continued Bernard, "none of us would actually be here were it not for Mestre. Rafael has heard this story many times but I will tell it to you now. You see, when my parents and I came to Rio from São Paulo, I was 13 and I didn't know anyone. Not one person. Then, one day, I was walking on the beach and I saw all these other kids doing amazing soccer skills.

They looked like they were having so much fun, so I asked their teacher—the man we know as Mestre—if I could join in. He said I could, and that's how I made all my friends here. And one special friend in particular..."

Bernard looked at Rafael for a second and then continued.

"One of the girls who was learning with Mestre was a brilliant soccer player, way better than me. I just thought she was the most amazing person I'd ever met. And, from that day, she and I were inseparable..."

Bernard stopped talking for a second. He seemed to drift off into the distance before focusing again on Jamie.

"Because of that—the fact that Stephania, Rafael's mom, and I met while practicing our skills—Mestre always says that Rafael is a child of soccer. It's a nice phrase, don't you think?"

Jamie nodded. And it was a nice phrase, but he couldn't help noticing the small tear that was rolling down Rafael's cheek. Jamie knew it was because he was missing his mom.

Bernard no doubt thought the same thing because he stood up and gave Rafael a really big hug and spoke some soft words to him in Portuguese.

"I'll leave you two to it," said Bernard softly. "And just have a little patience, Jamie. Mestre will know when you're ready."

***

Normally Jamie liked to stay up as late as possible. It was probably because he absolutely hated it when his mom told him he had to go to bed.

But tonight, Jamie actually wanted to go to bed. He wanted to read about the Legends of Brazilian Soccer in Mike's booklet.

"I'm going to bed," Jamie said, allowing himself an inward chuckle as he imagined his mom fainting at hearing him say those words.

"Yeah, me too," said Rafael, finally closing his notepad. "We were late today. We should get to Mestre early tomorrow. We have a lot to learn."

Jamie nodded and limped up the stairs. As he got to his bedroom door, he turned and looked downstairs to see Rafael pick up a framed photo by the banister and gaze at it.

Jamie had looked at that same photo earlier in the day. It was a picture of Bernard and Rafael's mom standing together outside the front door of the house. They were both so happy. Both smiling so broadly.

Jamie watched as Rafael delicately kissed the photo before placing it carefully back down on the table.

Jamie's text was only seven words long but he still squirmed a little when he sent it. He didn't like the mushy stuff. His mom knew that he hated it when she kissed him in front of other people. But seeing Rafael kiss the photo of his mom had made Jamie think.

Yes, they had lots of arguments and yes, sometimes she really got on his nerves, but he couldn't for one second imagine what his life would be like without her.

THE LEGENDS OF BRAZILIAN SOCCER

You would not believe how many wonderful players Brazil has had over the years, JJ. Zico, Sócrates, Ronaldo (the original one), Romário, Neymar...

The list is endless but, for me, by far the best are two attackers I used to watch when I was growing up. Their names were Pelé and Garrincha. Let me tell you, Jamie, these are two players whose names will live for ever. As people, they were as different from one another as you can imagine ... as soccer players, they had that quality that you and me always talk about and marvel at in the really best players – that extra little bit of magic.

Pelé was the son of a former professional soccer players whose career was cut short by injury (remind you of anyone?) and so he devoted his life to having the career that his dad never did. He ended up winning the World Cup three times and scoring a thousand professional goals.

He became an idol all over the world, respected as quite possibly THE greatest of all time. There is a famous story that goes that one day in Brazil some very dangerous armed robbers tried to steal an expensive-looking car. But when they saw that Pelé was the driver, they politely apologized, hid their weapons and went on their way! Like I said: Pelé is a legend - for everyone!

But so is Garrincha - in a completely different way. While Pelé was the perfect athlete, respected like a god all over the world, Garrincha suffered from a physical deformity from birth ... which became his greatest strength. He was born with bent legs.

PS I'm sure you'll learn your own
Portuguese while you're there. But here's a
word to kick you off. **Sim** - it means "yes".
So remember to shout that when you want
someone to pass you the ball!
Good luck, JJ ... and enjoy...

Rhythm of the Game

Monday, May 26th

"Good!" said Mestre, looking at Jamie's feet. Overnight the rawness had started to heal and was beginning to be replaced by a thick outer layer of skin. "Soon your feet will be ready."

"Soon?" asked Jamie.

"Today we make your body ready," announced Mestre, before he shouted something to one of the café owners on the beach. "Can you dance?"

What was going on now? Had Mike and Mestre somehow been in contact with each other? Jamie looked at Rafael for some assistance. But his friend, who was noting everything down in his pad, simply half-smiled, half-chuckled back in Jamie's direction. Rafael was offering no help.

Jamie shook his head vigorously. He hated dancing more than anything. He remembered his Aunt Judy trying to make him dance at one of his mom's birthday parties. She threw him around the room, pulling him and pushing him all the time, with her hot and sweaty arms bumping into him. It felt like some kind of physical attack.

"Rosária!" called Mestre towards the girl who Jamie saw balancing the ball on her head the day before. His deep voice seemed to coast along the sea breeze because, even with the distance, the girl immediately stopped the skill she was practicing, looked up and smiled.

Jamie did not notice quite how pretty she was yesterday; he had been too overwhelmed by her skill to observe anything else. Yet now, as she skipped along the sand towards Mestre, Jamie was absolutely struck by her.

The girl, who looked about 14, smiled at Mestre, giving him a hug and a kiss. Jamie heard her use the word "*Papa*". Even he knew what that meant.

A few quick words of Portuguese followed between them and then a nod from the girl to Mestre, after which she began walking towards Jamie.

Jamie felt his whole body freeze. He was unable to swallow or move.

"*Olá!* I'm Rosária," she said, sparkling brighter than any star Jamie had ever seen as she shook his hand.

"J-J-J... Jamie," Jamie stuttered. Welcome to Rafael's world, he thought to himself.

And then the music began. All of a sudden, from all of the cafés, there was loud samba music being blasted along the whole beach.

As if part of a game of musical chairs, as soon as they heard the sounds, practically everyone on the beach got up and began dancing! Out of nothing, there was now a full-scale party going on.

"Come," smiled Rosária, moving towards Jamie. "You dance with me."

"Ummm!" Jamie winced, his voice going higher than it was when he was five years old. "No, I'm OK, thanks!"

He tried to step away and find some place where he could hide, only to bump into the solid presence of Mestre, who was standing directly behind him.

"You want to learn how we play in Brazil?" he said. "Then you need rhythm."

With that, Rosária put her hands on Jamie's hips and started to guide his body to move in time with the beat. It felt seriously awkward. Especially with her dad watching.

He looked again at Rafael, who was now filming what was happening on his phone. Jamie shrugged and forced a smile at the camera, to which Rafael responded by giving Jamie a big thumbs up.

Jamie was so nervous. This was nothing like dancing with his Aunt Judy. This was a proper girl. He never
danced with a real girl like this. He bet if he ever tried
suggesting to Alex that they should dance together she
would probably have kicked him in the shins!

But now, here he was, dancing to Brazilian music on
the beach with one of the most beautiful girls he had
ever seen. And she was three years older than him!

"Sorry!" said Jamie. He stepped on Rosária's toes for
the fifth time in three minutes. Everyone else on the
beach was doing professional twists and turns, while
Jamie was moving like an Egyptian mummy, as though
his body was frozen in time.

"Close your eyes," Rosária said. "Forget everything,
OK? Hear only the music."

Jamie tried. He really did. But he just couldn't get it.
When Rosária moved left, he moved right. When she
took a step towards him, he did the same. Instead of
gliding smoothly across the sand, their bodies were
clashing and banging into each other like bumper cars
at the fair.

"It's no good," he said after ten minutes of torture. "I
don't have rhythm. Let's just accept it. Some of us, like
you, have it. Some of us, like me, don't, and nothing
you can do will change that. Now can we forget it and
start working on some skills?"

He started to turn away.

"Everyone has the rhythm!" laughed Rosária, clasping

Jamie's hot sweaty hand in her cool palm. "It's in there. We just have to find it."

Jamie watched Rafael march on. He had no choice but to follow.

Let Your Feet Feel the Beat

"Here," said Rosária. "Touch this. Put your hand on it."

Jamie knew that was what she said by reading her lips. He certainly couldn't hear the words themselves.

They were standing outside one of the beach cafés, directly next to a humongous speaker. Rosária had dragged him here and was now placing his hand on the enormous, vibrating sound system.

"Can you feel it now?" she shouted.

"Feel what?" roared Jamie, trying to make himself heard above the noise.

"The beat! You have been listening to the melody. Forget the melody. Your feet need to feel the beat!"

With that, she placed her hand on top of Jamie's and pressed them both down hard on the speaker.

The pulse of the music was making the speakers move, sending waves of strong vibrations through their hands.

"Can you feel it now?" she asked, pushing Jamie's hand down even harder on the speaker.

Jamie nodded.

"I can feel it!" Jamie shouted. "I can feel the beat insi—"

Rosária put her finger on Jamie's lips to stop him speaking.

Jamie carried on mumbling but Rosária wouldn't let any more words tumble from his mouth.

"Don't talk," she said. "Just relax. Just dance. Good… Goood!… *Ginga!*"

Jamie could have sworn the last word she said was "*ginga*". That was what the kids in the UK sometimes called him when they were being mean about his red hair.

He looked up at her accusingly but she was still smiling kindly back at him. She did not look as though she was teasing him now. In the midst of the loud music, he must have heard the word wrong.

He smiled back at her and made sure he concentrated on keeping the beat…

"OH. MY. GOD," Jamie said to Rafael, wiping the sweat from his forehead as he gulped down a whole bottle of water. The music just stopped. "How long have we been going?"

"About t-two hours," said Rafael.

"Two hours!" said Jamie, spitting out his drink.

"Well, how long did you think it had been?"

"I don't know, half-an-hour, maybe."

"Time flies when you're having fun, huh?"

Jamie nodded. It had been fun all right. He could see now why Mike had always dreamed of dancing the samba all night. Brazilians were experts at knowing how to enjoy themselves. At one point, while they were dancing, a whole group of people had even gathered around to watch Jamie and Rosária, applauding all of their moves.

"Look out," said Rafael. "She's c-coming over."

"*Obrigada*," said Rosária, giving Jamie the smallest of kisses on both of his cheeks.

Jamie smiled and nodded back to her. He didn't feel like a shy and nervous little boy any more.

"*Obrigada* yourself, Rosária," he said, trying to sound extra smooth as he ran his fingers through his hair. "So..."

"No, Jamie!" laughed Rosária. "Girls say *obrigada*, you say *obrigado*... unless you are a girl. You are not a girl, are you, Jamie?"

"No! Oh my God no!" said Jamie, his temporary coolness shattered in an instant. "I promise I'm not a girl, I just—"

But it was too late. Rosária was already making her way back to the skills area, leaving Jamie to ask himself two questions: did that all actually just happen?

And what on earth did any of it have to do with soccer?

Just Like Ronaldo

"You know," grinned Rafael. "I think you've got a thing for girls who play soccer!"

They were walking home from the beach and Jamie was still bouncing along to the rhythm inside his head.

"Shut up, Rafa!" he said, giving his companion a friendly shove for good measure.

"It's true! There's Alex at home, and now you obviously think Rosária is the most beautiful girl you've ever seen!"

"I said: shut up!" laughed Jamie.

"Don't worry, I'm just jealous—I didn't get a kiss, did I? And anyway, you're not the only one. Ronaldo was the same."

"Ronaldo?" said Jamie. "Which one?"

"The original Ronaldo. The Brazilian one. He once met this girl called Milene. She was phenomenal at soccer, I mean like record-breaking phenomenal. She once juggled the ball 55,000 times."

"Shut up!" Jamie repeated. "There is no way that's true."

"Swear on my life," said Rafael. "Look it up when we get home. Her name is Milene Domingues and she set that world record for juggling the ball when she was 17! And guess what else?"

"What?"

"She was a model."

"No way."

"Yes way. And guess what else? She played for the Brazil Women's National Team. And guess what else?"

"There's more?"

"Ronaldo married her!"

"I'm not surprised!" said Jamie.

"Yeah," laughed Rafael. "I mean, they got divorced in the end but when they were married they actually played soccer together. I bet you'd like that wouldn't you, Jamie—playing soccer with your wife!"

"I'd just like to play soccer with anyone at the moment," he said.

Although he had an outstanding day dancing on the beach, a part of Jamie remained disappointed. He still hadn't actually played soccer yet in Brazil and it was killing him.

"I mean, I'm not being funny or anything," said Jamie, turning the subject away from soccer-playing supermodels. "But do we even know that Mestre is that good at soccer himself? I haven't seen him kick a ball yet."

Rafael gave Jamie a withering look.

"You are my friend, Jamie," said Rafael. "But sometimes you ask all the wrong questions."

They were now passing through the streets where the poorer kids were playing soccer again.

"Hey!" Jamie said to Rafael, his face suddenly brightening. "This is perfect. I can play with these guys!"

Jamie put down his bag and went to do up his laces nice and tight. The soles of his feet still hurt a bit... but not enough to stop him playing. This would be great, playing with the street kids on their own turf...

"No," said Rafael, putting his hand on Jamie's shoulder. "It's not safe for you to play here."

"What are you talking about, not safe?" said Jamie. "They're just kids like us; that's what you said yesterday. They won't do anything to me."

"It's not the players," explained Rafael. "That is not the reason. Look at where they're playing."

Jamie looked at the ground that the kids were playing

on. Initially, he saw nothing wrong, but then when he looked closer, his eyes started to pick up the detail. The ground was covered in bits of stone, rocks and even animal bones. And yet the kids were still playing barefoot.

"Right," said Jamie, his voice dropping. The last thing he needed was to sprain his ankle on a rock and end up in the hospital. His mom would have a nervous breakdown. "Well, can we at least watch for a bit?"

"Of course," smiled Rafael, taking out his notepad.

Jamie and Rafael watched the street kids playing for about half-an-hour. Jamie saw how they deftly evaded the rocky debris and admired their touches of street skill as they nimbly dribbled past one another.

Towards the end of the game, the smallest, thinnest boy wearing the same old, ripped Brazil shirt had once again spotted Jamie and approached him. Again, he tugged at Jamie's Hawkstone shirt. Again, Jamie refused, but he smiled at the boy and looked into his eyes.

The boy's face was so dirty and his frame was painfully thin and yet his eyes were clear and expressive. It was an image that remained fixed in Jamie's mind.

"Rafa, can I ask you a question?" said Jamie, still thinking about the boy as they turned into the plush suburb where Bernard's house was.

"Go ahead," said Rafael.

"Well, if everyone in your country loves soccer, if all of Brazil is obsessed by the game and if there are lots of rich people in houses like this, then why do those kids have to play... like that?"

Rafael looked at Jamie. He seemed a little shocked.

"You are right, Jamie," said Rafael, shaking his head. "And you know, my mom always used to ask exactly the same question."

All in the Notepad
Monday, May 26th

Jamie looked into Rafael's room. His friend was sitting at his desk, lost in another world as he scribbled furiously in his notepad. In all the time that they had known each other, Jamie had still never seen him without it.

Jamie was desperate to know what Rafael wrote in that notepad. He knew it was to do with soccer because when, yesterday, Jamie had asked Rafael if he ever played soccer, Rafael said that he used to when he was younger—and that he was an OK player—but that now he preferred to study the game. Jamie had noticed that when Rafael said the word "study" he subconsciously tapped his notepad.

It was all in there, even though Jamie just didn't know

what it was. Part of him was tempted to steal the pad for a minute when Rafael wasn't looking just to sneak a peek at what was inside, but Jamie knew he would never do that. He would only ever see what was inside the notepad if Rafael let him.

Jamie went downstairs, noticing immediately how springy his feet felt against the carpet. The burns were nearly healed and it was almost as if the outer layer of skin had evolved into a new tougher, harder membrane that now covered the inner, more sensitive part of his foot.

"How's it going?" asked Bernard, who was sitting in the kitchen, as Jamie helped himself to a glass of milk from the fridge. The milk somehow tasted different from what he was used to at home—a little sweeter, perhaps.

"Eh, alright I guess," said Jamie. "It's been good and everything, but I haven't actually kicked a ball yet."

It was only when he'd finished speaking that Jamie realized that Bernard might not have been talking about soccer. He might have been referring to Rafael's stutter, wondering whether his son was any closer to speaking freely in public.

That was a difficult question to answer. On the face of it, there had been no progress: Rafael still wasn't speaking to anyone in public—or even his dad—without a stutter. Yet when it was just him and Jamie, it was now impossible to shut him up! The boy had turned into a complete chatterbox!

"Oh, by the way," said Bernard, changing the conversation. "You should go and get yourself ready. We're leaving in ten minutes."

"Huh?" said Jamie. "Where we going?"

"To watch some soccer," replied Bernard. "Some real Brazilian soccer."

Really at the Game

PALMEIRAS VS SANTOS
ESTADIO DO PACAEMBU
SÃO PAULO

The sound hit Jamie like a wall.

He was right in the middle of a sea of 40,000 soccer-crazed Brazilians, all of whom were singing, smiling and banging their drums, all ready for the beginning of the game. Palmeiras vs. Santos: two of the most famous teams in the history of Brazilian soccer.

As they took their seats, Jamie watched Bernard giving Rafael a big hug. It reminded him of when he and Mike went to watch Hawkstone. There was something special about going to soccer matches, something that brought people closer together. This must be the big event that they had to come home for, Jamie thought to himself. And he could understand why. To be here, at a top Brazilian soccer match, was well worth travelling across the globe.

Jamie looked around him. Men, women, boys and girls of all ages, all colors, all races—all singing and happy, all dressed in Palmeiras's famous white and green uniform. They had completely forgotten their normal lives. They were just here to enjoy the game. *This is a carnival of soccer*, Jamie thought. *And I'm part of it!*

Keeping to his agreement with Rafael, Jamie was shouting for Palmeiras just as loudly and passionately as if he had been at a Hawkstone match. And almost right from the kick-off, there was a lot for Jamie to cheer about; the match rained goals!

It seemed as though each time one of the sides scored, the other team would just go up to the other end and equalize. It was everything Jamie could have hoped for: goals, skills and celebrations. He was up from his seat every five minutes, clapping, roaring his approval and giving Rafael a massive high five and hug each time Palmeiras scored.

By half-time, the game was already 3-3, one of the highest-scoring 45 minutes Jamie had ever seen. Rafael was using the break to update his notepad while Bernard went to get them some drinks.

* * *

Everything was just about perfect. Jamie, however, was not smiling. In fact, there was something that had really started to annoy him and it was beginning to make him angry too: practically all the fans around him had been making fun of him throughout the first half.

Right from the moment they arrived, just as the game kicked off, and all the way through the match itself, many of the people sitting around Jamie had been shouting "*ginga*" at him.

Jamie didn't like it when he thought Rosária used that word at the beach and he liked it even less now.

He knew there weren't many people with bright red hair like him in Brazil and he accepted the fact that it made him look different to everyone else. But to single him out and shout "*ginga!*" at him really loudly and laugh and clap while they did, well, that was completely out of order. He could feel his anger rising again. He knew he had to say something; otherwise he might lose his temper.

"Can you please tell them to stop?" Jamie asked Bernard as soon as he came back with the drinks.

"I hate it. It's mean and I can't enjoy the game properly with them shouting '*ginga*' at me the whole time because of my hair."

Bernard and Rafael both looked at each other and raised their eyebrows.

"Do you want to tell him or shall I?" Bernard asked Rafael.

Rafael pointed to his dad. He started laughing.

"OK. It's not exactly what you think, Jamie," said Bernard. Even he was nearly smiling too. "In Brazil, *ginga* is nothing to do with the color of someone's hair. It means something else here. It is a very important word that we use to describe the skills, the joy, the personality needed in order to make beautiful soccer.

"We say *ginga* when Ronaldo cleverly dribbles past three defenders and the goalkeeper before back-heeling the ball into the net. *Ginga* is when Ronaldinho smiles before flicking the ball over your head and volleying it in, and *ginga* can also be the way you sway your hips when you are dancing…

"It is a rhythm, a feeling—a kind of joy—so when the fans are saying it, they are not talking about you, they are cheering for the players, to give them a mood to bring out the *ginga* in the air, to let it sweep from the stands to the pitch."

"Oh, right," said Jamie, suddenly feeling a little foolish. "Well, if it's not about me, I guess that's OK, then."

* * *

Once Jamie knew what *ginga* meant, he enjoyed the second half much better, and so did the Palmeiras fans, because after having gone 4-3 down, they managed to come back to win 5-4 in spectacular fashion.

When Arnaldo's winning bicycle-kick goal went in, Jamie actually thought one of his eardrums might burst, such was the noise generated by everyone within the stadium.

"*Gol! Gol! Gol! Gol! Gol! Gol! Gol! Gol! Gol! Gol! Gol! Gol! Gol! Gol! Gol! Arnaldo!!!! Gol! Gol! Gol! Gol! Gol! Gol! Gol! Gol! Gol! Gol! Gol!*" shouted the commentator, who was sitting a few seats back from Bernard and the boys. The man was going completely crazy.

Jamie and Rafael turned to look; he was standing up, his face was bright red and he screaming into his microphone, still repeating: "*Gol! Gol! Gol! Gol! Gol! Gol! Gol! Gol! Gol! Goooooooooooool!*"

He must have done it about 100 times. Jamie and Rafael laughed and tried to copy him. They got up to 40 before having to stop due to complete exhaustion.

As they made their way back to the car from the stadium amidst all the other fans, Jamie felt as if he was floating across the ground. Back home, when he tried to explain to people (other than Mike and Alex) how he felt about soccer, how much he loved the game, how it was in his mind the whole time, they didn't understand. They just told him things would change when he discovered girls. They had no idea.

But, here in Brazil, not only did everyone completely understand Jamie's love for soccer, they all felt exactly the same way!

Opening Up

"Thank you so much! That was the best game that I have ever seen in my life!" beamed Jamie when they got home.

It was also the longest car journey Jamie had been on since he moved to the UK—nearly five hours all the way back to Rio from São Paulo, though that was nothing compared to what he was used to in the States. It was now nearly 3:00am, but Jamie was still wide awake, and he wasn't the only one.

Sitting around the kitchen table, eating pastries filled with hot, creamy chicken (a dish called pastel frito de frango, Jamie learned), the three of them were still talking about the incredible game they witnessed. Or rather, Jamie was talking and the other two were listening because, while Bernard nodded and Rafael scribbled away in his notepad, Jamie unleashed a relentless review of every soccer-based thought that was popping into his head.

"Now I can say I've seen a top match in Brazil! Mike is going to go ballistic when I tell him!" he said proudly, almost shouting, even though the other two people in the room were sitting at the same table as him.

"And I can always say that I saw Arnaldo play when he was really young. You were right, Rafa—he was amazing! He'll definitely get signed by a European club in the next transfer window. Talk about technique! That bicycle kick was insane. I mean, how do you actually become that good? He was literally on another level!

"I'll tell you what I want to know, though," continued Jamie. "What did the Palmeiras manager do to change it when they went 4-3 down? It was like he switched the entire team formation and then they went and won 5-4. How did he do it?"

Jamie finally allowed himself a breath and a big gulp of water. Then he suddenly noticed Bernard looking at Rafael.

"Go on," said Bernard to his son. "Why don't you show him, Rafa?"

Rafael stopped writing in his notepad and looked up. There was a second of silence as he looked at his dad, then at Jamie and then back down at his notepad. He seemed to be weighing up the most important decision of his life.

And then, extremely slowly and extremely carefully,

Rafael got up, came to sit next to Jamie, and held open his notepad for Jamie to see the pages.

Jamie stared at what was in front of him. His eyes widened and his mouth hung open.

He was looking at some of the most advanced, analytical and complex soccer sketches that he had ever seen.

First 30 mins ends 3-3

Palmeiras - ○
4-2-1-3
2 holding midfielders
Wingbacks running down out wide.
10 Arnaldo - behind the striker but ineffective due to lack of the ball.

Santos - ●
4-3-3
inside forwards ie Mess; style
3 midfielders, 1 "holding"
Fullbacks important - need to run up and down the wing.

Formations are very attacking, free roles & expressive.

Palmeiras

Santos

RDC

Second 30 mins ends 4-3 to Santos

Palmeiras – ○
4-2-1-3 (same)

Santos – ●
5-3-2 (change)
3 defenders with 2 wingbacks.
Dominate midfield due to the extra
(3rd) man.

Palmeiras

Santos

RDC

Last 30 mins 5 - 4 - Full time How Palmeiras won it.

Palmeiras 2-3-2-3
Santos 5-3-2

Only 2 defenders (a gamble) but have
more numbers in the midfield to dominate possession. If Palmeiras have it
Santos can't score.

Key Change – 10 Arnaldo moved to
central attacking position, so all play
and chances come to him.

Magic Moment – Arnaldo's winning goal.
Intricate midfield passing. Jadson (3)
advances and crosses deep. Ball at
wrong height for Arnaldo, who changes
his body position, leaps into the air,
scissor kicks in top left corner! Gol!
Gol! Gol!

Across the pages were three images, representing the three thirty-minute phases that totaled the full 90-minute match they just watched. Each diagram depicted how the two teams were structurally set up for that period, detailing their formation, tactics and passing movements.

Together, the three drawings faultlessly reproduced the entire story of the game from a tactical point of view and explained just how Palmeiras pulled off a tactical masterstroke, enabling them to come back and win the game.

It was just about the most beautiful piece of work that Jamie had ever seen in his life. It was science, art and soccer all combined.

"Oh my God!" said Jamie, snatching the notepad out of Rafael's hands. "Let me see that!"

Jamie took hold of the notepad and flicked through the pages. Everything he saw was the same level. It was the work of a genius. Quickly, Jamie turned another page and saw himself. Or rather, a diagram of himself, with key analysis of all his strengths and weaknesses as a player.

"Rafa! Can I keep this for the night? It's ama—"

But then Jamie stopped talking. Because he saw Rafael's face.

"G-G-G-Give it b-b-b-b-b-back!" Rafael shouted, grabbing the notepad from Jamie, tearing one of the pages in the process.

Jamie looked at himself in the full-length mirror on the inside of the closet door. He was in his bedroom. There was just a thin wall separating him from Rafael. He had knocked on Rafael's door but it was locked and Rafael didn't respond to Jamie's pleas to let him come in. So Jamie went to his own bedroom instead.

It was such a nice, spacious room with a high ceiling, big closets and a beautiful wide bed. It reminded him of how he used to live in America, when he had everything he wanted, including his dad.

Jamie looked at his face in the reflection. The pale freckled skin. The darting blue eyes. Why did he hate himself sometimes? Why? Because he ruined everything.

Rafael was the kindest, most gentle kid he ever met. He trusted Jamie enough to open up to him like no one else and he invited Jamie into his world, made it possible for Jamie to come to Brazil, made a dream come true.

And how did Jamie repay him? By trying to take too much. By physically snatching the notepad away when Rafael only wanted him to look at it and breaking every element of trust that they established between themselves.

Jamie could hear Rafael crying next door. He tried to block it out. Instead, he looked again at his own face and watched as, in his mind's eye, it began to turn into his dad's face. Then he felt the anger coming again, building like a tidal wave. He forced himself to look again, just one more time. It was disgusting. He hated his own face. He wanted it gone.

The glass shattered upon the impact of Jamie's first, venomous kick. The shards flew everywhere and, before he knew it, Jamie was sitting on the bed, watching Bernard rush in to pick up the pieces.

"I bet you're wishing you never invited me here. I'm so sorry. I can't believe I broke the mirror," said Jamie, carefully helping Bernard to pick up the big pieces of broken glass. His anger was gone now. Just sadness about what he did remained.

"Look," Bernard said. "Forget about the mirror. There are just some things that you don't know. That notepad is very precious to Rafa. Just before she died, Stephania gave it to him because she knew how much he liked writing and drawing his soccer notes, so that's why he reacted like he did when you took it. It's not your fault but I think Rafa felt like you were taking a bit of her away. And I'm not sure he's ready to let her go yet."

Jamie shook his head. He knew about letting parents go—or, in his case, a dad letting him go—but that was still no excuse to have smashed the mirror.

"In fact, I think you should be proud," continued Bernard. "It's a very big deal for Rafa to open up his notepad and show it to someone. Aren't the drawings incredible?"

"Incredible," Jamie repeated. "And I ruined it."

"No," responded Bernard, shaking his head. "You're being too hard on yourself. You'll only ruin it if you stop or change now. Just get him talking again. That's how you can make up for it. When he is hurt, this is when he stops talking, but we can't let him go into his shell again. Now, more than ever, is the time for you to encourage Rafael to talk again."

Brothers

Tuesday, May 27th

"Your dad told me about the notepad..." said Jamie, hesitatingly. "That your mom gave it to you."

He and Rafael were walking to the beach as normal, but neither of them said a word to each other yet today.

They both ate their cereal in silence, Jamie stealing covert looks at his friend in the process. Rafael had dark bags under his eyes and Jamie suspected that he might not have slept all night.

He was trying to work out what to say to Rafael, how to earn his trust again, but it was difficult. Jamie wasn't great with words so he didn't say anything. Until now.

"I should never have tried to touch it," said Jamie.

Rafael nodded but he didn't look at Jamie. Bernard was right. He went back into his shell. They continued walking in silence.

Just one word. That was all Jamie needed. Rafael was talking so much since they got to Brazil, if he would just start talking again, Jamie was sure that they could pick up where they left off.

He reached deep into himself to look for something that might bring Rafa back. Then he remembered something that Mike always said: the more you give, the more you get.

"Can I tell you something I've never told anyone before?" asked Jamie, feeling a bundle of nerves begin to sprout within him.

Rafael nodded.

"Every day," Jamie hesitated, "when I wake up, the first thing that I do, before anything else, is pray that, one day, my dad will come back.

He talked quietly, and when he finished speaking, his mouth curved downwards. It was true—he did do that every day—and he never told anyone.

Rafael stopped walking and turned to look at Jamie. It was the kind of look that only brothers normally give each other.

Silence stood between them.

Jamie shook his head. A tear wet his eye.

"It's been nearly t-t-two years now," whispered

Rafael. "And you know, my d-dad hasn't smiled once—not properly—since m-my mom…"

Jamie thought back to Bernard's broad smile in that photo of him and Stephania at the house. It was such a big smile, that it looked as though it should last forever.

"Life sucks sometimes, doesn't it?" said Jamie. "I can only promise you one thing, Rafa. I will never ever let you down again."

31

Ready

Jamie and Mestre looked at each other, each bearing a steely glare, each unwilling to give way.

Jamie had once again asked to start working with the ball. Mestre had once again told him he was not ready.

Then Jamie felt the cord snap inside him. Ready? Why did he keep going on about being ready?!

"Fine!" said Jamie, picking up his stuff. "It doesn't even matter whether you think I'm ready because I don't need you! I'm in Brazil—the home of soccer—I can play soccer on the beach with anyone I want!"

With that, Jamie began stomping up the beach. His outburst didn't sooth his anger, it only inflamed it.

"You should come back," said Rafael, sprinting to try and keep up with Jamie. "You're making a mistake."

"The only mistake was wasting two whole days listening to his stupid ideas," snapped Jamie. "Like I'm going to go home and tell Alex and Mike: yeah, I was in Brazil but no, I didn't actually play soccer."

It was only the huge commotion that was occurring further up the beach that pulled Jamie out of his anger for a second. About 50 yards away, lots of people were making noise and shouting and clapping. They seemed to be aiming their attention in one direction, towards one particular person.

Jamie focused his eyes and made out a figure walking towards him down the beach. The person was being followed and cheered as he walked.

Indeed, it was the walk—the athletic grace of it—that gave away the person's identity. Jamie recognized him seconds before he could hear the cheers.

"Arnaldo! Arnaldo!" the people were singing, as the best young soccer player in all of Brazil walked down the beach.

Then something absolutely incredible happened: Arnaldo began to smile and wave in Jamie's direction!

Jamie could not believe it. This was way beyond his wildest dreams.

He smiled and waved back as the heroic figure drew nearer still... and then watched as Arnaldo walked past him.

It wasn't Jamie that Arnaldo was waving at.

Jamie turned around to see where Arnaldo was heading. Straight towards Mestre. What did Arnaldo want with the old man?

"Mestre!!" Arnaldo was now shouting, quickening his pace to give the Master a high five. "*Meu amigo!*"

Mestre and Arnaldo give each other a huge hug and immediately began laughing together. It was like a child greeting his favorite uncle.

Jamie shook his head in utter disbelief.

"Can we talk to him, Rafa?" he asked. "Can we talk to Arnaldo?"

"Well, that depends," said Rafael. "Last thing I remember is you shouting your mouth off at the man who taught him everything he knows!"

Meeting the Man

There's so much I want to ask you!" said Jamie, feeling his body tingle with excitement. "That magic in your play, please tell me how you get it!"

Mestre and Arnaldo were sitting on a couple of deck-chairs watching the kids by the sea perfecting their skills. When Jamie apologized for losing his temper, Mestre had just laughed and said, "It's good. This is what a soccer player needs: passion!"

Mestre explained that ten years ago Arnaldo was just like Jamie and the other kids, one of Mestre's students on the beach.

Arnaldo himself nodded.

"Eh..." Arnaldo said, looking at Jamie. "You learn with Mestre now, yes?"

Jamie nodded enthusiastically but, inside, he was full

of embarrassment. He couldn't believe that a few minutes ago he was prepared to turn his back on Mestre. This was the man who taught Arnaldo, and Jamie was annoyed with him enough to leave! What a waste it would have been if he stormed off. What a mistake. Maybe Alex and his mom were right; perhaps he did need to work on keeping his temper under control.

"And you have been running on the beach?"

"Sure have," Jamie grinned.

"And you have been dancing?"

"Yup," confirmed Jamie.

Arnaldo began laughing. He stood up and started doing some samba moves in front of Mestre. He even tried to pull Mestre up from his seat to dance too but Mestre was not interested.

"Mestre!" said Arnaldo, now laughing even harder. "So now it is time for him to play footvolley?"

Mestre got to his feet and smiled.

"OK," he said finally. "The American boy has passion. So now we see if he is ready."

Mestre and his daughter, Rosária, were on one side of the net, warming up, with Arnaldo waiting for Jamie to join him on the other side. Jamie was on his way; he was just getting some final instructions from Rafael, who had asked if he could have a minute to tell Jamie all the rules.

"Footvolley is basically a mixture between volleyball and soccer," he explained. "There is a court marked out in the sand, which you can see, and there is a net with two players on each side. In this case, it's you and Arnaldo versus Mestre and Rosária."

Jamie grinned. He loved it when Rafael said the words "you and Arnaldo".

"Listen, Jamie, this is important!" said Rafael. "There are lots of people watching, so you are going to want to play well. You can use any part of your body to control the ball and get it over the net apart from your hands. So, that basically means your feet, chest and head."

"Got it," Jamie said.

Looking at the intensity in Rafael's eyes, he suddenly felt as though he were being given a pre-match team-talk by a top coach. He realized again how much he liked and respected Rafael. He was so happy that they were talking again after what had happened last night.

"And remember," said Rafael. "Because you can't use your hands, it's very difficult to spike the ball, so some of these rallies will go on for a very long time."

Jamie nodded again, shook Rafael's hand, took his place on the court and high-fived Arnaldo. If he was completely honest, Jamie wasn't that worried or nervous because alongside him, as his partner, he had one of the best young soccer players in the world. All Jamie had to do, he reasoned, was try to set the ball up for

Arnaldo and this would be a pretty simple victory.

Not for the first time in his life, Jamie could not have been more wrong.

Golden Touch

The ball dropped perfectly, just over the net, and set-tled smoothly into the sand. It was struck with such sweet softness that it seemed to drop lightly towards the sand like a falling leaf.

Jamie and Arnaldo both collapsed, panting like wild dogs. Mestre had taunted and teased them by keeping every rally going for such a long time that, by the end, they were begging for it to be over.

Jamie ran and scampered as far and as fast as he could. Arnaldo had some unbelievable touches but none of them compared to the control of the ball that Mestre demonstrated.

Every single touch of the ball he took was pure gold, including this last one, when Mestre deftly flicked it just over the net with the outside of his foot to win the game for him and Rosária.

Jamie felt a hand grab him and pull him up from the ground.

It was Arnaldo. He still wore the same smile that he had before the game.

"Don't worry that we lose," he grinned as he and Jamie shook hands with their opponents. "This is why we call him O Mestre!"

Jamie nodded. For the first time since he arrived on the beach, he genuinely understood the truth of the situation.

On the other side of that net was a living, breathing master of soccer.

"He wouldn't tell me who he really was," revealed Jamie. "His real story..."

He and Rafael were just turning into the road of Rafael's house. Even though he lost at footvolley, Jamie was feeling much better. After all, he finally kicked a ball! Yet this one question was still bugging him.

"After the game and once we all took our photo with Arnaldo, I went up to Mestre by myself and said to him, 'Your touch is better than any player I have ever seen, even the ones at Barça and Madrid. Why hasn't the whole world heard of you?'"

"And let me guess," laughed Rafael. "Mestre didn't tell you his story?"

"No," said Jamie. "He just looked at me and said

people have the wrong idea about practice and training. They think to train until your body can't train anymore is the right way. He said that way was wrong. That was the way you got injured. He said what he believes is that you must train at the right time, in the right way, with people who can show you the right things. That is how you become a better soccer player."

"Yup," nodded Rafael. "Makes sense to me. You know, people say that they have never seen Mestre injured. Not one day. And he's been playing and coaching soccer on that beach for thirty years."

"Come on then," appealed Jamie. "You've got to tell me his story, Rafa. You must know. How did he get so good? Who is he?"

"He is exactly who he says he is," smiled Rafael, as though he knew more than he was prepared to tell Jamie. "He's the man who will show you the secrets of the Brazilian skills. He is 'The Master.'"

Night Mail

From:	**Alex Crawford**
To:	**Jamie Johnson**
Date:	**May 28th, 2:24 AM**
Subject:	**Hey**

How's it going out there? Tell me stuff! By the way, I bumped into Ms. Vetterlein in town today and she told me doesn't think she can play in the T v S game! Says Hawkstone's Women's Team have got a Cup Final that weekend and she can't risk it! Result! Say hi to Rafael for me.
A

From: Jamie Johnson
To: Alex Crawford
Date: May 28th, 2:28 AM
Subject: The MOST amazing thing in the world EVER

OMG, Alex, can't believe you emailed me now – I was literally JUST about to email you... You will not believe this! Today at the beach, WE MET ARNALDO!!!
He's the best young player in Brazil and he is so cool. He's got this whole Mohawk thing going on with his hair... Anyway!!! We played this soccer volleyball game and I was on THE SAME SIDE as Arnaldo! Just me and him. We lost (I didn't realize at the time, but there's a guy on the beach who's some kind of legend or something and he's going to teach me Brazilian skills tomorrow) but anyway, it didn't matter, me and him were so cool together, just high fiving the whole time!
Got a photo too, just in case no one believes me! Sending it with this email – let me know what you think. Can't wait to see you and start planning our tactics for Teachers vs Students. Love that Ms. Vetterlein's not playing! Maybe I should ask my mate Arnaldo to come and play for us?!
JJ

From: Alex Crawford
To: Jamie Johnson
Date: May 28th, 2:32 AM
Subject: Re: The MOST amazing thing in the world EVER

Awesome!! Definitely get him to play for us! Imagine Pratley's face when we turn up with Arnaldo on our side! ROFL just thinking about it!!
Who's the girl?

From: Jamie Johnson
To: Alex Crawford
Date: May 28th, 2:33 AM
Subject: Re: The MOST amazing thing in the world EVER

That's Rosária, the legend's daughter. Amazing at soccer and she's taught me how to dance too! Got some serious moves now!

From: Alex Crawford
To: Jamie Johnson
Date: May 28th, 2:34 AM
Subject: Re: The MOST amazing thing in the world EVER

How nice for you both

From: Jamie Johnson
To: Alex Crawford
Date: May 28th, 2:35 AM
Subject: Re: The MOST amazing thing in the world EVER

Don't be like that, Alex! She's a really nice girl. Please don't get mad at me.

From: Alex Crawford
To: Jamie Johnson
Date: May 28th, 2:52 AM
Subject: Re: The MOST amazing thing in the world EVER

Ha! Only pulling your leg! She seems really nice. Anyway, you can do what you want. You're not my boyfriend.
Yet.

Up in the Air

"There are many different types of soccer," said Mestre, his powerful, firm hand resting on Jamie's shoulder. "The beach is different from the rest because here it is difficult to dribble in the sand. Here, everything is about keeping the ball in the air. But you take these lessons from the beach and they work in any soccer. You understand?"

"Yes, Mestre."

"Good. So now you try."

Without warning, Mestre volleyed a soccer ball hard at Jamie, who instinctively chested it up into the air and began juggling with both feet. He had just passed his first test of Brazilian beach soccer.

Soon, Rosária came to join him, and then three more players. They formed a small circle on the wet part of the sand right next to the sea. They were playing the most simple of soccer games—keeping the ball up. Each player was allowed just one touch with any part of their body (except for their hands) and, collectively, their aim was to keep the ball in the air for as long as possible.

By watching the other players, Jamie realized that they used their shoulders, heels, thighs and knees just as much as their feet. Each part of the body had its own shape and way of connecting with the ball. For example, the knee and heel were hard, giving good power and distance, while the thigh and chest were soft, offering more control.

Also new to Jamie was the fact that they seemed to use the outside of their foot when touching the ball as much as the instep; not only did it allow the players to get so much more spin on the ball but it looked like more fun too!

Above everything, though, the key was to never give up. Every ball was retrievable.

"You can make that one!" Rosária said to Jamie on one occasion that he let the ball bounce into the sand.

"But it was too far away," appealed Jamie, sorry to have let the other players down. They had kept it up for 104 touches. "I would have needed to dive face-first into the sand to keep that one up!"

"Yes!" said Rosária. "And what is the problem with that?!"

It was true. Jamie watched how the other players

chased every ball down, diving into the air, running into the sea, leaping into the sand to kick, head or chest the ball back to a waiting member of the team.

The best part of it was that no one ever got injured because the sand or the water was always there to break their fall.

Jamie realized this when he made his first run into the sea, chasing down a ball at full speed, skipping into the water and then launching himself into the air, producing a bicycle kick—his trademark move—to arrow the ball back behind him to where the rest of the players were standing.

After he made contact with the ball, his whole body plunged into the refreshing blue Brazilian sea. It was like a cool, cleansing shower. Jamie blew the bubbles out of his nose and then, feeling his feet touch the sand, pushed himself back up and out of the water in one powerful movement.

He rose, refreshed, from the sea and then sprinted back on to the beach to continue the game.

As he did so, he saw Mestre nodding and smiling.

Now Jamie got it. Now he understood.

Or at least he was starting to.

One Last Trick

Saturday, May 31st – three days later

"I can't believe it," Jamie said to Mestre. "Ever since I've been playing with you guys, the time has gone by in a flash. I can't believe I have to fly home later tonight."

For the last three days, every second on the beach had been filled with soccer. All manner of games had been played: footvolley, keeping the ball up in the air, beach soccer. In each one the principle was the same —controlling the ball with every part of the body and keeping it in the air for as long as possible.

Initially, Jamie found it difficult. In the UK, all of his coaches always told Jamie the same thing: "Keep the ball on the ground!"

That was how the Europeans did it; the Spanish, the Italians generally passed the ball on the ground. This was different. This was about keeping it up, keeping it alive, by any means and any skill possible.

However, with each second, with each hour and with each day, Jamie got better and better. By now, Jamie's last day, he developed the skill to use every part of his body in his play. There was not a ball that he didn't believe he could keep in the air somehow.

It had reached the point that the Brazilian beachgoers were now used to seeing the small, pale American boy sprinting like a madman into the sea or diving head-first into the sand to flick, kick or head the ball, just to keep a game going. Yes, it meant he got a face full of sand about ten times a day, but he could not have cared less.

Mestre was standing on the beach, looking at the sea, with Jamie juggling a ball alongside him.

"We are always here," said Mestre. "You can come and see us again."

Jamie nodded, but something inside told him that this was a once-in-a-lifetime trip.

"If I don't," said Jamie, catching the ball for a second, "can you teach me one last trick? A special one? You see, when I get home, I'm going to play in a huge match at school and I'll be up against an extremely difficult opponent. I'll need something magical to beat him."

Mestre turned and looked at Jamie. Although they

were getting closer and Mestre seemed to be happy with Jamie's progress, Jamie could still never tell what he was thinking. And he had never seen this look in Mestre's eyes either.

"*A Mágica,*" Mestre said after a while. "Rafael told you about *A Mágica?*"

They both turned and looked at Rafael who, as always, was making notes in his pad. He worked just as hard as Jamie over the last few days—in a different way.

"No," said Jamie. "He hasn't told me anything. It was just a question I thought of now, I promise."

"OK, then! It is your last day—I will do it," said Mestre, standing up and walking over to a game of beach soccer that was happening further down by the sea. As he walked over, the other players all stopped and smiled and began debating which side would take Mestre.

Perhaps sensing what was about to happen, Rafael came and sat down next to Jamie and, for once, closed his notepad and set his eyes on the match in front of them.

"Do you know what he's going to do?" asked Jamie.

"Maybe," smiled Rafael. "But I've only heard about it. I've never actually seen it."

A Mágica

The first five minutes of the game were not dissimilar to the other games of beach soccer that Jamie watched over the last couple of days: small dribbles through the sand, chips to teammates, acrobatic headers and volleys. And lots of smiles.

Then, with almost no warning, Mestre did something that seemed to turn the whole game of soccer on its head. Literally.

In the middle of the match, with the ball at his feet, Mestre flicked it up from the ground on to his head. He then proceeded to run past every single member of the opposition team while bouncing the ball on top of his forehead.

When he got to the goal, he let the ball drop from his head and volleyed it home.

All of the players in the game and Jamie and Rafael, watching from the sidelines, stood and clapped. It was both the most daring and effective bit of skill that Jamie had ever seen.

"What was that?" shouted Jamie. "He just dribbled the whole field with the ball on his head!"

"Yup," smiled Rafael, excitedly opening his notepad to start drawing. "And because the ball was on his head, no one could tackle him."

While Rafael was working, Jamie stood up and did the only thing in the world he could possibly think of doing. He tried to replicate the skill he just witnessed.

"Don't worry," said Mestre, walking past Jamie back to his seat. The beach soccer game just finished and Jamie failed to do the skill—for the 20th time. In each attempt, he managed to get the ball on his head, but it fell off as soon as he tried to walk with it, let alone run.

"You will not be able to do it," stated Mestre. He was speaking as a matter of fact rather than as a boast. "All my students have tried to do it—even Arnaldo—but no one is able. That is why I call it *A Mágica*."

"But I want to do it!" said Jamie. "It's amazing; impossible to defend against. Please teach me!"

Mestre shook his head. "It's impossible," he said. "It takes so much time and we have none."

Jamie felt a hand on his shoulder and looked around. He was surprised to see that Bernard had come to pick him and Rafael up. They were flying home later that evening; perhaps he wanted to save time.

Mestre smiled and nodded to Bernard. They said a few words to each other that Jamie could not understand and then Mestre gave Bernard a hug.

Now Mestre held out his strong hand for Jamie to shake.

"Good luck," he said. "You have learned the skills of the beach well. One day, if you come back, perhaps I can teach you *A Mágica*. Otherwise, it is impossible."

Jamie smiled and shook Mestre's hand firmly. It was strange. When he had first arrived at the beach, Jamie thought that Mestre was the complete opposite of Mike, and yet now, somehow, he reminded Jamie of his grandpa. Perhaps just the Brazilian version.

"Thank you, Mestre," Jamie said. "I will remember and practice everything you taught me."

And it was true. Although he only had a few days to learn from Mestre, the skills that he picked up on that beach—how to use every part of his body, how to play with rhythm and imagination—would stay with Jamie forever.

But you're wrong about one thing, Mestre, Jamie thought as the soccer computer in his head replayed the magical move that the master of skills had just shown him. *Nothing's impossible...*

A New Brazil

Bernard, Jamie and Rafael arrived outside a brand new building.

Bernard and Rafael took a deep breath as they looked at the construction.

"Are you ready?" Bernard asked, taking Rafael's hand in his.

Rafael nodded his head.

Then they began to walk.

When he had picked the boys up from the beach, Bernard explained to Jamie that, before they flew home, there was something they had to do, somewhere they had to go. This was the reason that he and Rafael had to come back to Brazil this week.

"But I thought you came back home to watch the

Palmeiras match?" Jamie said.

"No," said Bernard, shaking his head. "We are home for something different. It has taken time to build it, but now we can show you."

As they opened the doors, Jamie thought he saw Rafael and Bernard's eyes glisten with emotion. Then all three of them walked inside.

As soon as they entered, Jamie realized that this was not just any old building. It was a gym, housing a completely new soccer court. The floor was so clean, it was evident that no one had ever played on it.

After a few minutes, streams of people began to arrive. Each one of them came to give both Rafael and Bernard a hug and then take their place, standing all around the soccer court.

Soon, the gym was almost entirely full, and it included all the faces that Jamie saw during his time in Brazil— even the kids from the street were there.

It was strange because it looked as if this was some kind of celebration and yet not one person was smiling. In Brazil, as Jamie was beginning to find out, this was highly unusual.

It was only when Rafael strode forward into the center of the court that Jamie began to have some idea what this was all about.

Rafael's hand was visibly trembling as he pulled the cord to separate the drapes that were covering a plaque that was set into the wall.

Even though he didn't understand all the words, Jamie caught his breath as he read what was engraved on the plaque.

ϘARA STEPHANIA DA CRUZ

ELA ACREDITAVA QUE O ESPORTE
PODE CONSTRUIR UM NOVO BRASIL

De Bernard E Rafael

After he unveiled the plaque, Rafael took out a piece of paper, cleared his throat and began reading a small speech. Or at least he tried. His stutter was so bad and he was so emotional that after a few seconds, Bernard went to join him and together they began speaking, Bernard pausing each time his son stuttered so that they could complete the words in unison.

Jamie felt as though he might cry. He could see how upset Rafael was. Then he felt someone's presence next to him. It was Rosária. She and Mestre had just arrived.

"They are talking about Rafael's mom," she explained. "She was a psychologist and she worked with lots of children all around our city. Rich and poor kids. Everyone. She always said that sports were a way to heal the mind and she believed that all the kids should have somewhere to play together and so that is what Bernard and Rafael have built. This is for her. This was her dream."

Jamie nodded. He looked at Rafael and Bernard, who were standing next to each other, holding each other's hands, bravely fighting back the tears.

Jamie felt a tear of his own run down his cheek. He remembered how one day Rafael tried to describe to him how it felt to have a stutter.

"When you stutter, trying to get the word out is like reaching for something that is always out of your grasp," he had said.

It seemed to Jamie that the saddest part of all was that Stephania da Cruz could not help the one boy who really needed her most.

Jamie wiped away the tear and tried to reach for a smile.

"What does the sign say?" he asked Rosária.

"In English, it says *For Stephania da Cruz: She believed sport could build a new Brazil.*"

Caneta

Jamie looked at the small, thin boy and felt something between anger and respect.

This boy was the same kid, wearing the old, faded Brazil jersey, that Jamie had seen playing in the *favela* every day and always wearing that same shirt.

Now they were playing against one another in the first-ever game of futsal in the new Stephania da Cruz gym.

After Bernard made his own speech and the gym was officially opened, all of the kids present—some from the beach, some from the *favelas* and some from the richer suburbs—were invited to take part.

And it just so happened that Jamie had the misfortune to be placed on the opposing side to the boy in the Brazil shirt. That boy had already nutmegged Jamie, on purpose, three times during the game.

Now he was standing, looking at Jamie with the most mischievous grin possible.

Not that the kid was Jamie's only problem. This was futsal, not soccer, and even though Mike's booklet told him about the smaller ball and goal, it didn't prepare him for the level of speed and skill this game was played at. Everything seemed to be happening at 100 miles per hour. Jamie felt dizzy with the intensity of the action.

Time and again, when he had the ball, Jamie was taking too long and he got caught in possession. Then, when the other team launched their rapid counter-attacks, Jamie was either out of the game or, worse still, nutmegged by the little boy from the streets.

Finally, to make Jamie's embarrassment complete, not only was he playing on the same side as Rosária—and feeling thoroughly frustrated by his inability to impress her—but he was also aware that Mestre was among the big crowd of Brazilians watching the game.

Seeing Mestre had given Jamie an idea, though. Perhaps there was one truly special way for him to show the people watching how good he was.

"*Sim!*" Jamie shouted, remembering Mike's piece of advice to him in his booklet.

Rosária just collected the ball and turned past a player to get herself an inch of space. Without looking up, Rosária heard Jamie's shout and provided him with an instant pass.

Controlling the ball on his thigh, Jamie knew this was the moment to try it. He flicked the ball into the air and began attempting to softly head the ball to himself as he ran forward.

It was a brave move.

And Jamie's attempted *A Mágica* was over after approximately a second.

He tripped himself up and fell flat on his face, allowing the opposition to score straight away.

The crowd on the touchline could not help but laugh and point at Mestre. They all knew *A Mágica* was his trademark move and that no one else could replicate it.

Jamie sat, embarrassed, on the floor of the gym. But he was no quitter; he accepted Rosária's firm hand of support and got back up to his feet.

As he jogged into his position waiting for the game to restart, Jamie ran past Mestre. He couldn't help but notice that Mestre was staring straight at him with the exact same look that he gave Jamie on that first morning at the beach. He was focusing angrily at Jamie's sneakers.

Jamie could almost hear Mestre talking to him.

You must touch the ball with your feet. Football starts with the foot...

Hurriedly, Jamie took off his sneakers and his socks to reveal his bare feet. Then he looked again at Mestre.

Mestre was now smiling and so was Rosária.

Just as when they danced at the beach, it was Rosária who was about to lead Jamie, to show him the way. Except this time she used her skill.

With the ball back in play and with Rosária in possession, one of the opposition players approached her to try and make a tackle. Rosária drew him towards her, dragging the ball back towards her own body using the sole of her foot—and then, as soon as the player got too close, she flicked the ball up and over his head, dancing around the other side, to meet the ball on the drop with a spellbinding volley, which dipped right into the top corner of the goal.

The skill was mesmerizing, and Jamie could not help but applaud. He was in awe of Rosária. He wanted to play like that.

"We are inside but we can still play as if we are by the sea," she said, giving Jamie a high five. "No matter where you are or who you play against, you can still play with the rhythm and the joy. It's time for you to bring the beach skills back. OK?"

Time to Dance

With Rosária's words still ringing in his ear, Jamie closed his eyes. For just one second, he had to shut off everything else in the world. He had to find the beat inside him.

He felt his heart pumping and he listened to its rhythm. Jamie's heart beat for soccer.

The next time he received the ball, Jamie produced a double drag-back with his first two touches.

"*Olé!*" the crowd shouted.

Then Jamie nutmegged his very next opponent before keeping possession by flicking the ball back to Rosária.

"*Caneta!*" "*Ginga!*" the spectators clapped.

Jamie could feel his cheeks burning with pride. He produced a *caneta*, in Brazil, and, even better, the player he nutmegged had been the boy with the Brazilian jersey!

Jamie just nutmegged the tiny prince of the nutmegs!

Now Jamie was starting to get respect. All of his different attributes as a soccer player were coming to the fore. He had the sure touch from the beach, he had the extra fitness that running on the sand every day gave him, he was picking up futsal's quickness of movement and shrewd flicks, and on top of that, he still retained what he always had—his trademark rocket-like pace and a fiery determination to never give up, to keep going for every second of the game.

It was a unique combination and, when all of these qualities came together, it meant that Jamie was almost impossible to stop.

"*Ginga!*" the crowd shouted again and again as Jamie began beating players at will. The more they shouted, the more confident he became. They were shouting another word at him too. It began with 'F' and seemed to end with 'O'. Jamie could not quite make it out, but he didn't care. They could shout whatever they wanted. Right now, it was all about the game.

Starting to believe that they quite possibly had a very special player on their side, all of his teammates began giving the ball to Jamie whenever they could. And now he could see Rosária preparing to flick another pass his way.

Instantly, Jamie controlled the ball on his chest,

deftly flicked it past a player using his thigh, and then knocked it down the line to use his pace.

He scorched past the defender and, from a wide angle, took on an audacious curling shot. However, rather than using his instep, Jamie went with the outside of his bare left foot, aiming to curl the ball towards the far corner. The ball started off way outside the line of the far post but, with the amount of extra spin he was able to generate on the ball by using the outside of his foot, it started to come back in, curling more and more the longer it spent in the air.

The goalkeeper dived high and wide, using all his elasticity to reach the ball, but there was never going be any chance of stopping it. Jamie's shot was destined to nestle in the top corner of the net from the moment he struck it.

It flew in. *Goooooooool!* Jamie shouted wildly in his head.

It was a phenomenal strike and Jamie raised his hands in the air to take the applause. He even attempted something that resembled a little Brazilian samba dance!

Again the crowd clapped; again they shouted that strange word beginning with 'F' at Jamie. Now it seemed everyone was talking about the pale American boy with the colorful Brazilian skills.

In the middle of the spectators, even Mestre was impressed by what he was witnessing.

He put his hand on Rafael's shoulder, wagged his finger and said with a coach's pride:

"I knew the boy was ready."

At the end of the game, Jamie shook hands with every player on the court. He even got a hug and two kisses on the cheek from Rosária, who actually seemed sad that he was leaving.

Jamie was still pinching himself when the thin boy in the Brazilian shirt came up to him. During the game, he and Jamie had enjoyed a titanic battle of nutmegs. The boy beat Jamie five times and Jamie returned the favor to him twice—and all the while the boy never stopped smiling.

They high-fived, and although language was a problem, their mutual respect of each other's talent broke through the barrier.

Then the boy began tugging at Jamie's shirt again. Just as he did on Jamie's first day in Brazil.

Jamie looked down at his Hawkstone shirt. He thought long and hard. Then he had an idea.

Jamie pointed to boy's Brazil jersey. The shirt was tiny, faded, tattered and ripped, but it was a Brazil soccer shirt from the streets of Brazil.

There and then, both boys took off their shirts and swapped. As he handed over his Hawkstone jersey, for a second Jamie wondered whether he was doing the right thing. That shirt meant the world to him. But he also had a warm feeling in his stomach that told him this was something he would never regret.

Although it was extremely tight on him, Jamie put on the Brazil shirt and walked off the brand new futsal court. He cast his mind forward and imagined the future. Instead of having to play in the stony, dusty, dirty streets, every one of the kids from around the neighborhood—rich and poor—would all be able to play here, whenever they wanted.

Jamie hoped that, looking down from somewhere, Stephania da Cruz would be very proud.

Fire in Your Feet

Jamie slid down the window and breathed in the smooth Brazilian night air. Would he ever come back? Would anyone here remember the American kid who came over to play with the Brazilians? Certainly, Jamie would never forget them.

"Hey!" said Jamie, suddenly remembering what he meant to ask Bernard since the game ended earlier that evening. "You know when we were playing? Every time I got the ball and started to dribble, all of the people watching started shouting something—I think it began with 'F'. Do you know what it was?"

"*Foguinho* is what they were calling you," Bernard answered from the driver's seat. "It is their nickname for you."

For a second the car went silent. The bright lights of

the airport loomed into sight just ahead of them. And then it clicked for Jamie.

"What? You mean I have a Brazilian nickname?!" he shouted so loudly that Bernard almost crashed the car. "I have a Brazilian nickname! Me, Jamie Johnson, has a Brazilian nickname! Oh my God! That's amazing! Wait until I tell Mike and Alex! *Foguinho... Foguinho*! I love it! Hi, I'm Jamie Johnson, but you can call me *Foguinho!*"

"D-d-on't you w-want to know what it means?" asked Rafael, looking at his friend, who appeared to have gone slightly crazy, just repeating the word Foguinho over and over again.

"It means something too?!" yelled Jamie. "Oh, that's even better. This just keeps getting better!! Yes, please tell me! What does my nickname mean?"

"It m-means L-Little Fire."

"Little Fire!! How cool is that? Little Fire – I love it! Is that because I'm small and fast and I burn past the defenders?" asked Jamie.

"Y-y-y-es, p-p-robably," smiled Rafael, who was laughing now. "And m-m-aybe also b-b-because of this!"

Rafael pointed to Jamie's bright red hair.

"Y-y-ou h-have f-f-fire in your f-f-eet, f-f-ire in your heart and f-f-ire on your head!"

"Yeah," laughed Jamie. "Good point!"

Then, with his excitement at its peak, and, despite the fact that he never did anything like it before in his life, Jamie suddenly burst into a rap.

"*Foguinho is my name,*

Soccer is my game,

I'll take you on, down the line,

I'll skill you up, each and every time!

Don't try to stop me,

Don't even try to foul me,

It makes no difference, how many men surround me.

I'll skill you up,

I'll burn you down,

My. Name. Is. Foguinho.

Little Fire just came to town!"

Heading Home

Jamie scratched his scalp and looked at his fingernails. They were full of sand. Normally that might be a bit disgusting, but, right now, Jamie looked at it a different way. He liked the idea that he was bringing some of Brazil back home in, or rather on, his head.

It wasn't all he was bringing back either. He had the magic from Brazil—from Mestre's school of skill—inside him now and he was determined to keep and practice those skills every day before the big match at the end of the school year. When that day came, he wanted to be ready, Jamie thought, borrowing the phrase that Mestre always seemed to use.

He smiled to himself and looked at Rafael. His friend was leaning his head against the airplane window with his mouth wide open and his tongue hanging out to the side. Jamie couldn't believe that Rafael slept for practically the whole flight home.

What made it even more frustrating was that Rafael had promised to tell Jamie the true story of Mestre on the plane—who he really was and how he really got those skills—and then, as soon as they ate their meal, he fell fast asleep!

Jamie thought about his time with Mestre. He thought about Rosária and the other kids on the beach and he thought about the amazing night that Bernard took Jamie and Rafael to see Palmeiras play. Jamie now understood that, all the time they were there, Bernard was preparing for the opening of the futsal gym and yet he still made time to be the best host for Jamie.

Jamie looked across at Bernard, who was making some architectural sketches, his face as serious as ever.

Jamie unbuckled his seatbelt, stood up and walked over to him.

"Thank you so much for inviting me," said Jamie. "I just hope I didn't disappoint you."

Bernard put down his pencil. "Disappoint me? How?"

"Part of the reason you invited me was to help Rafa get over his stutter in public and it hasn't happened."

Bernard shook his head. "Jamie, we invited you because you are a true friend to Rafa," he said. "I didn't expect you to cure him. Just to have fun with him. And I know you two did that."

Jamie nodded. "It was the best time of my entire

life," he said. "And I'm so sorry about your mirror!"

Bernard didn't respond. Instead, he did something that no man besides Mike had done to Jamie since his dad went to jail.

He gave Jamie a hug.

PART THREE

Talking Tactics

Wednesday. July 16th

Six and a half weeks later

The day before the Teachers vs Students match...

"You need to know your opposition," Mike said, staring at the three young, hopeful faces in front of him. "So what Rafael has been doing: watching the teachers train, working out their formation, that is exactly the right thing to do."

Jamie, Alex and Rafael looked at one another and smiled. For weeks now, everything they did was geared towards this game. As soon as they were all back together in school after spring break, Jamie, Alex and Rafael held try-outs to see which three players would be joining Jamie and Alex on the sixth grade students' team.

There were lots of good players to choose from—both

boys and girls—and as captain, Jamie found the process of telling the other kids that they didn't make it into the team very difficult. In the end, though, Rafael, put it best when he said, "You can't make an omelet without breaking some eggs."

And so, finally, the trio had settled on the following team and formation: Alex in goal, the Talbot twins in defense, Aaron Cody in midfield and Jamie in attack.

Not only was Rafael present at every one of the students' training sessions in the park—always kneeling by the side of the pitch, making notes in his pad and passing on information and tactics to the team via Jamie —he also made sure he saw all of the teachers' training sessions on the playground too. He would conceal himself from Pratley's view by hiding behind the cars and memorizing everything he saw. He compiled comprehensive fact-files on every member of the teachers' team, all the while devising his own set of special tactics to beat them.

Ultimately, Rafael's tactics revolved around one simple idea: the teachers were playing with Mr. Duggins in defense. He was a fat man and an extremely slow runner; Mr. Pratley had been forced to pick him when Ms. Vetterlein insisted she couldn't play in the Teachers vs. Students match because of the Cup Final she was expected to play in for Hawkstone the following weekend.

Once news of this leaked, Rafael pounced on Duggins' presence in defense as the teachers' weak point and decided that the students should exploit this weakness with their strongest, most dangerous threat: Jamie Johnson.

Rafael knew that if Jamie took on Duggins whenever he got the ball, Jamie would beat him every time. It would unlock the defense. It would unlock the whole game.

If Jamie was the most powerful weapon on the pitch, Rafael was the mastermind off it. He told every player their individual responsibilities and they all knew the overall team tactics by heart. All the work was done.

Everything was set and now, the night before the game itself, Jamie, Alex and Rafael came to see the man who knew more about winning big matches than all of them put together: Mike Johnson.

"Have your tactics but also be prepared to change," Mike told them. "A match evolves during its course. It never stays the same. If you are too regimented—just sticking to your original plan—you will break. You have to be flexible to change with the circumstances."

While Jamie and Alex listened intently, Rafael nodded and wrote furiously into his notepad. He soaked up every piece of soccer information that was ever offered to him.

"And above all, if you defeat your opponents, never gloat. The time of your greatest triumph is the time to show some humility. That goes for life as well as soccer."

Mike took a big gulp of coffee and let his words sink in.

"Good luck, you guys," he said. "Go make it happen."

He smiled to himself and looked at Rafael. His friend was leaning his head against the airplane window with his mouth wide open and his tongue hanging out to the side.

The Truth of the Legend

Jamie walked home that night with an extra spring in his step.

After they left Mike's, he, Alex and Rafael had a group hug. They knew that the next time they would all see one another would be the day of the game itself. The day they hoped to lift that gleaming school trophy.

And Jamie knew that he was ready.

Everything about the way his body felt told him so. Not just because he was training with Alex and the rest of the team every afternoon, carefully keeping to Rafael's set plan and tactics, but also because, even after he left them, every night he was continuing his own search for soccer perfection.

Taking his mind back to Brazil, he devoted countless hours working on every single skill that he learned over there. While he practiced, he imagined Mestre standing—arms folded—nodding occasionally, guiding Jamie in the art and skill of Brazilian brilliance. Once, when attempting *A Mágica*, he even managed to walk a few steps with the ball balancing on his head! He called Rafael right away to see if he could somehow get the message back to Mestre in Brazil!

Jamie was surprised at how often he thought of Mestre since they were back home. His presence seemed to be with Jamie all the time. Perhaps it was because of the story of his life. Rafael finally told Jamie the truth about Mestre the day after they got back home from Brazil, and it was a story Jamie could not forget.

"Come on then," Jamie had said to Rafael. "You said it was a good story. And it must be: to get skills like that, to be able to do *A Mágica*. Go on, tell me. What's the deal with Mestre?"

"Mestre was brought up in the *favelas*, one of the poorest of them all," Rafael began. "He was a brilliant young soccer player but his family had no money and he had no education so, as a young boy, he found other ways to survive. He pickpocketed people, stole from shops, that kind of thing. But then, when he got older, it became more serious, and when he was 19, he was sent to prison for 13 years.

"In those 13 years, he was let out for only one hour each day. The rest of the day, it was just him in that cell alone. He only had one possession: a tiny little ping-pong ball. He spent ten hours every day for 13 years practicing his touch with that little ping-pong ball. It was that little ping-pong ball that gave him all his skills. By the time he was released, it was too late for him to become a soccer player, but even though he couldn't be a professional, he now had the touch of a magician. He went to prison a boy, a young criminal. He came out as *O Mestre*."

"Wow," said Jamie. "That's sad, but it's incredible, and it makes sense too. If you can control a ping-pong ball in a prison cell, no wonder you'll have become a master with a normal ball by the time you get out. That is some story."

Jamie paused for a moment. He wondered how his dad was doing in jail. If he was coping. If he was safe. They were the same thoughts and fears that haunted Jamie every day.

No matter how much he tried to ignore them, they were always there, lingering like demons beneath the surface of his mind.

"It is an amazing story," Rafael said, sensing where Jamie's thoughts had gone. "And my dad says it shows that prison does not have to be the end. Sometimes it can also be a beginning.

"When Mestre got out, he wanted to start again and to put his skills to good use by teaching others. And, as you know, he has helped at least one boy become a professional soccer player."

Jamie nodded. He thought about Arnaldo a lot, too.

"No wonder you have so much respect for O Mestre," Jamie said. "He's an amazing man."

"True enough," smiled Rafael. "And, of course, he also has a very pretty daughter!"

Let Down

Thursday, July 17th
Match Day: 8:04am

"You're not coming, are you?"

Just one look at his mom's face told Jamie everything he needed to know.

"Jamie, they just called me this morning. They're short. They need me."

"I knew it! I knew this was going to happen! Why didn't you just say you weren't going to come in the first place?" he stormed. He wanted her to be there so much. He was so upset, so desperately disappointed. He just had no way of handling it.

"I wanted to come, Jamie. You know I would love to, but this is my job. I don't have a choice. You'll still have Mike there."

"Exactly!" shouted Jamie. "Because he's the only one that cares about me!"

"Jamie!" his mom pleaded. "Jamie! Wait!"

But he was gone, slamming the door shut so hard behind him that their entire little house shuddered.

"What's wrong with you?" asked Alex, who was waiting for Jamie outside her house. Her excitement for the match had changed to concern as soon as she saw Jamie.

Jamie shrugged and shook his head. He had been on a high ever since he got back from Brazil. He felt so relaxed and confident, probably the happiest he had ever been—at least since moving to the UK. And yet now, on this day of all days, he could only feel anger. The worst part was that, somewhere in his mind, he had been expecting this. Whenever he was really looking forward to something, he was always let down in the end.

"Do you have your uniform?" Alex asked.

"Of course I do!" snapped Jamie.

Alex stared at him. He never talked to her like this.

"Look!" he shouted, opening his bag for her to see. "Everything apart from socks and shin guards. Happy now?"

"Don't you want to get your socks and shin guards?

"Not if it means going back home!" barked Jamie.

The Big Warm-Up
Match Day: 11:07am

Aaron Cody, Dexter and Kane Talbot and Jamie Johnson all lined up on the edge of the area to take their shots at goal. Alex Crawford bounced in anticipation between the posts and Rafael da Cruz looked on watchfully from behind the goal.

It was recess and, while they were practicing, the rest of the kids were placing chairs around the playground's edge. The whole school would be watching later and lots of parents would too. Everything had to be in place. Very soon, the school trophy would be brought out if its cabinet. That's when things started to get really exciting.

Now it was time for the final warm-up. The last chance to loosen muscles and work on tactics before kick-off, which was just over three hours away.

Jamie could sense the eyes of the other kids on him. It was the same when he watched Hawkstone warm up: he always focused on the star player, Max Armstrong, analyzing his every movement. He knew the other, younger kids were doing that to him right now.

Jamie watched and waited his turn as Cody coolly slotted his shot home, followed by Talbot, who blasted his effort into the roof of the net. Talbot was next—he saw his strike brilliantly saved down to the left by Crawford.

And then it was Jamie's turn. All the kids putting the chairs down stopped what they were doing in order to watch.

Jamie waited, ready on the edge of the area as Aaron softly rolled a cross along the ground towards him.

Jamie saw the ball coming. He analyzed its speed and direction, gathered all his strength and then went for a major blast of a strike.

To his and everyone else's horror, he missed the ball entirely. A complete air shot.

"Give me another one," he shouted quickly, before anyone had a chance to react. "There was something in my eye."

So, from the other side of the pitch, Dexter spun over a perfect cross. It was a juicy pass, drifting through the air, just begging to be hit.

Jamie saw the ball coming and this time elected to take it on the volley. He swiveled, planted his right foot firmly in the ground, and shaped his body for a left-foot strike. Then he attacked the ball with a violent swipe.

This time he made contact all right but in the worst possible way. Jamie ballooned the ball—not only over the goal, but also over the entire school building.

Everyone watched it sail skywards and then drop into the parking lot next to the school entrance. The ball must have hit the roof of a car because there was an audible thud followed by the loud wail of an alarm going off.

It was not just the car that was alarmed.

Some of the kids gasped. Most were shocked into silence. This was Jamie Johnson. This was the best player in the school. This was three hours before kick-off. This was a major problem.

"What's wrong, JJ?" asked Alex as she and Rafael came to talk to their friend.

"Is it n-nerves? Are y-you OK?" asked Rafael.

Jamie hung his head.

He was anything but OK.

Quick Getaway
Match Day: 1:32pm

Everything was set. Just lunch and then kick-off.

"Where are you going?" asked Alex. "We need our energy."

She was keeping an eye on Jamie today. She could tell something was wrong.

And now, just as they were going into lunch, he seemed to be slipping away, going somewhere else.

"Have to go and do something," was all Jamie would say. "Don't worry. I'll be back for the match."

Jamie waited until everyone went to lunch. Then he went into the bathroom, took off his shirt and pants, put on his soccer gear and put his school clothes back on over the top.

It was a boiling hot day and Jamie now had on way too many layers but he didn't care. All he cared about was that Mike had got the text he sent an hour ago.

Those two practice shots Jamie took at recess were horrific. He knew that there was no way he could play in this game while his argument with his mom that morning was still on his mind. He had to make up with her. It was the only way for him to get himself together. He just hoped Mike would be able to help him.

Jamie walked out of the back exit of the school, looked at his watch, checked that no one was looking and then jumped over the school fence as quickly as he could.

He saw the car and sprinted across the road to get in. He checked again. Thankfully, no one had seen him.

Mike Johnson smiled and patted Jamie on the knee.

"I need to be back in 30 minutes," said Jamie.

Mike smiled and started the car.

"We'll have you back in 25."

Ready for the Whistle
Match Day: 2:12pm

The whole school was waiting.

Rafael was going out of his mind, tearing through the pages of his notepad, trying to work out a different tactical plan.

Alex was kicking the goalposts in frustration.

And Mr. Pratley was smiling. Just three minutes left until kick-off.

Jamie had been missing for more than 30 minutes by now. It was clear to everyone that he had chickened out. He was a no-show.

But then, finally, he appeared... just moments before kick-off.

"What?" Jamie smiled nonchalantly at Alex. "I told

you I'd be back for the match!"

Jamie sprinted on to the field, in his full uniform, missing only his shin guards and socks, ready to take the kick-off for the students' team.

As Mr. Karenza made Jamie and Pratley shake hands before the start, Jamie looked around at all the people who were watching: every single student and a bunch of parents too.

Jamie did not have either of his parents there to watch. But that was OK, now that he made up with his mom.

She was completely taken by surprise, not just to see Jamie and Mike suddenly appear at the hospital while she was working, but with the huge bouquet of flowers they had for her too.

"I just wanted to say I'm sorry, Mom," Jamie said. "I understand that you can't come to the game because you have to work and I know that the whole reason you work is for me, for us. I was an idiot to shout at you. Will you forgive me, please?"

Jamie's mom gave him the warmest hug in the world.

"Of course I forgive you, Jamie," she said.

Jamie felt the biggest sense of relief. Nothing stressed him out more than arguing with his mom.

"Thank you," he smiled. "I really don't think I could have played properly in this match otherwise."

Then Mike said, "JJ and I have a little idea, Karen.

I just called the stables up at Morris Farm. Would you believe June Leon is still working there? She says they've got a lovely big horse who's perfect for you. His name is Ivan and she says you can go up there anytime you like. We thought you would like to ride again."

Jamie's mom let a few tears fall down her face. She thanked them and said she would visit the stables that weekend. Then she told them to get back to school as quickly as possible. She knew how important this game was.

"Just make sure you score the winning goal for me, Jamie," she whispered in her son's ear.

49

The Plan Comes Together

THE BIG GAME
TEAM LINE-UPS

Referee: Mr. Karenza

Teachers	Students
Mr. McManus (GK)	Alex Crawford (GK)
Mr. Duggins	Dexter Talbot
Mr. Glyn	Kane Talbot
Mr. Regis	Aaron Cody
Mr. Pratley (C)	Jamie Johnson (C)

20 minute halves

Right from the first whistle, Rafael's plan kicked into action.

Jamie made sure that he was marked by Mr. Duggins and, whenever he got the ball, he simply destroyed him for pace.

The first goal was a perfect example. Dexter Talbot tackled Mr. Regis and, without a moment's hesitation, slid the ball through to Jamie. Jamie could feel that Mr. Duggins was close behind him so he let the ball go past on purpose. Then it was just a straight race between him and Duggins for the ball.

Jamie motored past him, barely having to go into his turbo-gear to ease away. Mr. McManus came out of his goal to close down the angles but Jamie just breezed past him too. He looked around and saw that he was so far clear that he even waited for Mr. Duggins to chug back towards his own goal.

Jamie watched Duggins sprinting towards him before, at the very last minute, swerving his body out of the way so Duggins crashed straight into the goalpost. Then Jamie simply walked the ball into the net.

The plan was working like clockwork. The students were ahead within five minutes!

TEACHERS 0 − 1 STUDENTS
J. JOHNSON, 4'

On the touchline, the kids roared and so did some of their supporters, Mike the loudest among them.

"That's my boy, JJ!" he shouted proudly as Jamie sprinted over to celebrate with him.

"That one's for Garrincha!" yelled Jamie, leaping into the air to give Mike a high five.

Meanwhile, standing just in front of Bernard, Rafael calmly made some extra notes in his pad. The game was unfolding just as he hoped—but he knew there was still a long way to go.

Now, with confidence coursing through their side, the students started to play some slick one-touch passing soccer, all with the objective of releasing Jamie when the time was right.

It was Alex who spotted the next opportunity. She slung a quick pass out to Jamie, who controlled the ball softly on his thigh before standing up straight to see which direction Mr. Duggins was going to come from.

Immediately, he saw Mr. Duggins loping towards him. There was only a second to think, but Jamie smiled because he knew exactly what he was going to do. He waited until Mr. Duggins was close enough and then, ever so sneakily, Jamie flicked the ball right between Mr. Duggins' legs.

"*Caneta!*" Mike and Bernard shouted from the sideline.

Mr. Duggins tried to turn around but his big wobbly body could not contend with the pace at which Jamie was moving. Instead of spinning and chasing after Jamie, Mr. Duggins just toppled to the ground.

Jamie sprinted on, flicked the ball into the air and volleyed a pass over to Aaron Cody, who met the cross with a perfect first-time finish. This was the playground of Wheatlands School but it could have been a beach in Brazil!

Now the kids were really starting to understand that this could happen. The students might actually beat the teachers.

From somewhere behind one of the goals, a chant began. Soon, all the kids around the playground were singing:

"Pratley! What's the score?

Pratley, Pratley what's the score?"

Jamie punched the air. His team was right on track to create school history and become the first Students team to ever beat the Teachers.

TEACHERS 0 – 2 STUDENTS
J. JOHNSON, 4'
A. CODY, 9'

"He needs help!" shouted Mr. Pratley. He was crouching down beside Mr. Duggins and seemed to be whispering something in his ear.

"It's my left—I mean my right knee," Duggins was saying, grimacing as he clutched it. "I fell when Johnson nutmegged me."

"Can you go in goal and give it five minutes?" asked Mr. Karenza, now also on the scene. "Maybe it'll get better."

"No," said Mr. Duggins, almost before Mr. Karenza had finished the question. "I'm afraid I can't continue. I'll need to be substituted."

"Yes, he'll have to be substituted," repeated Mr. Pratley. "He'll have to come off and we'll have to get a replacement."

"But there are no subs," said Mr. Karenza. "Who can you get?"

Jamie and Alex, who had now joined the group around Duggins, looked at each other. They knew the answer before Pratley had even said it.

"It has to be Ms. Vetterlein," smiled Mr. Pratley.

THE MOVE

"I'm sorry," said Ms. Vetterlein apologetically.

She was standing watching the game from the sidelines like the rest of the school.

"But we've got a Cup Final this weekend and I promised my manager I wouldn't play today."

Jamie and Alex breathed a huge sigh of relief. They had immediately argued that it would be completely unfair if the teachers got Ms. Vetterlein—she was a semi-professional, after all.

"Of course you can play," shouted Pratley. "You'll have to."

For a second there was widespread shouting on and off the field as all the players, students and spectators had their say.

"If you could play, Ms. Vetterlein, it really would help us out greatly," said Mr. Karenza finally, attempting to restore some order to proceedings. "If the teachers' team doesn't have enough players then we'll have to abandon the match, which would be such a shame for everyone."

Ms. Vetterlein looked at Pratley and then again at Mr. Karenza.

"We'd really appreciate it," Mr. Karenza repeated.

"OK, why not?" she said finally. "What harm can it do? Where do you want me to play, Mr. Pratley?"

With that, she jogged enthusiastically on to the playground. She didn't even have to change because she was already wearing her tracksuit and sneakers.

As she joined the game, a sense of fear swept around the students' team. Ms. Vetterlein was some player. Although she was nice and cheery around school, all the kids had seen her play for Hawkstone ladies; on the field she was a natural-born predator. One chance equaled one goal.

"You go up front," Pratley told Ms. Vetterlein. "I'll take care of Johnson at the back."

It was the kind of substitution that could alter the whole face of the game. It was almost as if Pratley had planned the entire thing from the very beginning.

***

Rafael da Cruz sprinted around the outside of the field to crouch down behind the goal. When he got there, he tore through his pad, searching desperately for other plans, other formations.

The kids just could not deal with Ms. Vetterlein's movement. She seemed to have the ability to slip into the most dangerous positions unmarked. She had Rafael extremely worried, and rightly so.

Three times in the span of seven minutes she worked herself free inside the box, and on each occasion, she finished with the cold touch of an assassin. She struck her first goal to Alex's left, her second to Alex's right and, for her hat-trick, she chipped the ball over Alex's desperate reach.

Ms. Vetterlein had turned the game on its head in what seemed like the flick of a switch.

TEACHERS 3 — 2 STUDENTS
H. VETTERLEIN, 10, 14, 17   J.JOHNSON, 4'
A. CODY, 9'

While Rafael was wracking his brain for tactical solutions, Pratley milked all of the goals to their fullest, cheering loudly right in front of the kids, before leading his teammates in airplane-style celebrations.

Watching Pratley's sickening smile as he pranced around the playground like an overgrown baby almost made Jamie puke in his own mouth.

Yet that wasn't even the biggest of Jamie's problems. With Ms. Vetterlein now up front, Pratley had dropped back into defense to replace Duggins, and he was an entirely different opponent for Jamie to counter.

"Go on," Pratley had said to Jamie during their first one-on-one. "Knock it past me and then run after it. Kick and chase, but where's your skill?"

Each time Jamie got the ball and prodded it down the line to run after, Pratley always seemed to be there, either anticipating Jamie's run or else fouling him to make sure he couldn't get away. Suddenly, it looked like Jamie had been eradicated as a threat to the teachers.

Then, with half-time fast approaching, Ms. Vetterlein went on another direct run right into the heart of the students' territory. She twisted the Talbot twins inside and out, rendering them dizzy and bewildered, before somehow finding a powerfully accurate shot from the acutest of angles.

Before anyone could react, the ball was in the back of the net once more.

"Ha ha ha!!!" screamed Pratley, joyously. "This is too easy!"

Mr. Karenza blew his whistle. "4–2 to the teachers," he announced. "And that's half-time!"

"No goal!" shouted Alex, suddenly rushing out from her area to confront Mr. Karenza. She had a mixture of anger and panic etched on her face. "Sir! The ball went in through the side-netting—it's no goal!"

"Oh, be quiet, Crawford!" said Pratley. "Stop being such a bad loser!"

Pratley bounced up to Ms. Vetterlein to give her a high five.

"Put it there, partner!" he shouted, cheesily.

However, Ms. Vetterlein left Pratley hanging.

"She's right, Mr. Karenza," said Ms. Vetterlein. "It went in through that hole in the side netting. The goal shouldn't stand."

"What!" screamed Pratley at his teammate. "What are you doing?!"

Mr. Karenza looked at the little gap in the side of the net. Then he looked again at Ms. Vetterlein for a second before blowing his whistle.

"My mistake," he shouted. "That was no goal. The score remains 3–2 and that is half-time!"

How Do We Stop Vetterlein?

TEACHERS 3 − 2 STUDENTS
H.VETTERLEIN, 10, 14, 17   **J. JOHNSON, 4'**
                                   A. CODY, 9'

"Come on, guys!" said Jamie, looking at each one of his teammates individually. "We're only one down, and we could have been two down! This is the exact time we have to step it up. We have to fight harder, run faster and play even better.

"If we want this—if we want to be the first students team to win this game—the next 20 minutes have to be the best soccer we've ever played! We can do this!"

Jamie bit into his orange and tried to keep his body calm. Did he say enough? Had he inspired his teammates to make a comeback? Could they stop the teachers now that Ms. Vetterlein was playing?

Jamie watched his teammates nod back at him. They were supporting him as their captain; they were behind him. But they also needed more. They needed a plan.

"Rafael," said Jamie. "How do we do it?"

The new plan was clear and concise. With Vetter-lein now on the field, Rafael knew that it left them far too exposed at the back. They had to revert to a more defensive formation. Rafael decided they would switch to three men at the back with just Jamie in midfield. He even instructed Dexter and Kane Talbot to both man-mark Ms. Vetterlein.

Even through his stutter, everyone clearly understood their role. Rafael was still fluent in soccer.

"This whole plan relies on you and your discipline," Rafael said privately to Jamie just before the re-start.

"The most important thing is that, when we don't have the ball, you hold," he warned. "You have to keep your defensive position, Jamie, because if you leave that position, you are out of the game and our whole plan is destroyed."

Taking the Bait

The tactics worked. Playing three at the back with both Talbot twins marking and Jamie cutting off the supply line in the midfield starved Vetterlein of the ammunition she required.

Yet it also meant that the students had no attacking threat themselves. On the rare occasions that Jamie even got the ball, he was so isolated that he had to try and take on all the teachers by himself. It was impossible.

All the while, the minutes were still ticking by and the students were still losing 3–2.

Then, with four minutes left to go, Pratley, who was in possession of the ball, did something very unusual. He did nothing. Nothing at all.

He did not try a pass or a dribble. He did not attempt

a shot. He just stood, with his foot resting on top of the ball, waiting.

Jamie looked at Rafael.

"Hold!" Rafael mouthed urgently.

"3–2 to us, isn't it, Johnson?" Pratley asked. "So we don't have to attack. You have to come and get it."

With that, Pratley started juggling the ball and whistling.

"Boooooooo!" jeered all the kids on the sidelines. "Time-waster!!!"

But Pratley didn't care. He knew his team just needed to keep hold of the ball for three more minutes and the game would be over.

Jamie could feel his frustration starting to boil into hot anger.

He knew Rafael was still mouthing that he should hold, that he should stay in position, but it was no use. The more Jamie looked at Pratley's smarmy face and heard his stupid whistling, the more the rage was growing. Then the cord snapped.

Jamie left his holding position in the midfield and tore up the pitch at rocket speed, straight towards Pratley.

This was exactly what Pratley had been waiting for. With Jamie now having vacated the midfield space, Pratley immediately clicked into action, playing a quick one–two with Ms. Vetterlein. Then he dashed into the gap that Jamie left behind.

Jamie watched in horror as Pratley advanced towards the goal and drew back his foot to strike.

Jamie knew if Pratley scored, it would all be his fault. He couldn't let this happen.

Just as Pratley was about to shoot the ball home, Jamie flew into the air and took him down from behind. He had no other option.

Mr. Karenza blew his whistle hard and loud. Meanwhile Pratley just laid on the ground. It was so obvious, he didn't need to try and sell the penalty to the referee.

Then he slowly stood up with a huge satisfied smile on his face. Jamie Johnson fell into his trap. He took the bait.

Mr. Karenza picked up the ball and walked over to Jamie. "I'm not going to end the school year with a sending-off," said Mr. Karenza. "This is supposed to be a friendly game, Jamie, so that is a yellow card for you."

Then Mr. Karenza raised his voice for everyone to hear.

"Penalty for the teachers," he shouted. "Two minutes left!"

53

The Penalty

"I'm taking this one!" said Pratley, snatching the ball from Ms. Vetterlein.

"Are you sure?" she said calmly. "You do know I've never mis—"

"Of course I'm sure," he snorted. "You've had your goals. This one's mine."

With that, he placed the ball down on the spot and took four deliberate, slow steps backwards. Then he walked back to the ball, picked it up and replaced it in exactly the same position.

"Boooooooo!" shouted all the kids watching the game. "He's time-wasting again, Ref!!"

"Hurry it up please, Colin," said Mr. Karenza, blowing his whistle again.

Jamie prayed to all the gods of soccer as he watched Alex jumping around on the spot, springing into the air to prepare herself to face Pratley's penalty.

Everything is riding on this one moment, Jamie thought. Please, let her do this.

Then it went deadly quiet as everyone in the school saw Mr. Pratley stride purposefully towards the goal. It was this to win it.

Pratley readied himself, took aim and then fired. He thumped the ball as hard as he could, sending it shooting through the air, heading straight for the top corner of the net.

"Goal!" he shouted as soon as the ball left his foot.

However, Mr. Pratley did not have any idea quite how good a goalkeeper Alexandra Crawford really was.

Alex flew into the air like an eagle, stretching every muscle and sinew of her body towards the ball. She reached out her hand and, with the very tip of her finger, clawed the speeding ball on to the post.

"Woooaaah!" reacted the crowd as they saw the ball rebound from the post and roll along the goal-line before Alex leapt across to smother it.

"Yes!" shouted Jamie, sprinting over to Alex and giving her a huge high five. "That was incredible! You saved it! And you saved me—if they had scored, it would have been completely my fault!"

"What did you expect?" said Alex, laughing. "Now get

up the field, will you? There's only a few seconds left! "

TEACHERS 3 – 2 STUDENTS
H. VETTERLEIN, 10, 14, 17   J. JOHNSON, 4'
A. CODY, 9'

Aaron Cody tried one final, long, desperate pass out to Jamie on the wing. He over hit it, though, and the ball was heading frustratingly out of play behind the teachers' goal.

Aaron Cody dropped his head. So too did the Talbot Twins, Alex Crawford, Rafael, Bernard, Mike and everyone else who wanted the kids to win. They all knew that, once the ball went out of play, Mr. McManus only had to do a little time wasting with the resulting goal-kick and it would all be over.

The same result as always: the teachers beating the students.

However, one of the kids was thinking of something else, somewhere entirely different. Seeing the ball loop past him, Jamie's mind reverted to the beach, to juggling the ball with the rest of Mestre's skills students by the water's edge.

What would he have done had he still been there? How would he have reacted to the ball threatening to get away from him?

Jamie's body answered the question before his mind.

He raced after the flying ball, dashing across the hard playground cement just as if he were scampering across the boiling hot sand towards the soothing cool blue sea.

Jamie knew that the only way he could keep the ball alive was to meet it in the air.

He launched himself towards the ball and, in mid-air, managed a perfect bicycle kick to not only keep the ball in play but also volley it hard and fast back across the goal.

The ball scorched through the air, crashing smack into the back of Pratley's head, rebounding directly towards the goal at unstoppable speed. Mr. McManus was motionless as the ball bulleted past him. Pratley, with a little help from Jamie's bicycle kick, produced the perfect goal-scoring header. The only problem for him was that it was in the wrong goal! Pratley had scored an own goal!

"Yes!" roared Jamie, pumping his fist.

"No!" wailed Pratley.

"Full time!" announced Mr. Karenza.

TEACHERS 3 – 3 STUDENTS

H.VETTERLEIN, 10, 14, 17   J. JOHNSON, 4'

A. CODY, 9'

C. PRATLEY, 40'

All Over?

It may have been full time but that did not mean that this game was over. Not just yet.

"OK," said Mr. Karenza, looking at his watch. "The match is drawn 3–3, but we need to have a winner in this game, so now it'll be next goal wins!"

Mr. Karenza blew his whistle to restart the game.

Jamie stood bent over with his hands on his thighs, panting. He had given everything, every ounce of energy that every cell in his body had to offer.

He was also paying the price for the fact that the 'field' they were playing on was actually the hard playground cement rather than soft beach sand. He looked down and saw the cuts, grazes and gashes that now made his left leg look like something from a horror movie.

He had nothing left.

And then the chants started.

Softly at first, but getting louder and louder.

"*One Jamie Johnson,*" some of the kids started to sing to encourage him. "*There's only one Jamie Johh-hhnsonn.*"

Meanwhile, on the other side of the playground, the other kids began shouting: "*USA! USA! USA!*"

Everyone then began clapping their hands, cheering louder and louder for Jamie.

Jamie looked at all the kids in the school. He knew how desperately they wanted to put one over on the teachers, how much they wanted to win this game.

First Jamie felt the buzz. Then his heart started to pump a little faster. He sensed the strength start to flood back into his body and felt the skills coming through, ready to shine.

He was ready for one last push.

Jamie immediately called for the ball and sprinted straight at Pratley. He felt strong and confident.

With futsal-like speed, he flicked the ball between Pratley's legs for his second nutmeg of the game and was just about to run through for a shot on goal when Pratley pulled him back by his shirt to stop Jamie getting away.

But Mr. Karenza waved play on. He didn't see it.

The force was with Jamie now. He was motoring. He

felt good but, on each occasion that he threatened to get through on goal, Pratley simply did the same thing —he tugged Jamie back by the shirt to prevent the opportunity.

Finally, on the third occasion, Mr. Karenza intervened.

"That's a booking for you, Mr. Pratley," he said, brandishing a yellow card.

"About time!" snapped Jamie. "He keeps pulling my shirt. If he does it again you have send him off!"

At this outburst, Pratley and Mr. Karenza immediately turned their attention to Jamie, both frowning at him with an expression that suggested Jamie had overstepped the mark.

"You've got a short memory, Jamie!" said Mr. Karenza, referring to the bad foul that Jamie himself committed erlier. "I told you I didn't intend on sending anyone off today."

But what did that mean? That Pratley had free rein to keep pulling Jamie's shirt for the rest of the match? If that was the case, then Jamie was finished.

Jamie looked across to Mike in despair. As always, Mike's demeanor was calm and positive. He pointed to his head and told Jamie to think.

And that was exactly what Jamie did. He searched his mind for an answer, for a solution that would allow him to get away from Pratley—even if it was just once. Quickly, he dug deep into the depths of his brain until he saw a small glimmer of light.

Without saying a word to anyone, Jamie reached his arms over his shoulders and pulled off his top, chucking it to the ground by the side of the playing area.

The people watching the game looked at Jamie. Some thought he took off his shirt as an act of disgust at Pratley's constant fouling. Others believed it was because of the heat.

They were wrong.

Jamie removed his shirt because he wanted to expose the other jersey he had, all along, been wearing underneath.

The item of clothing he now displayed to everyone was very old. It was dirty too. It had holes in it and it was so tight Jamie could barely breathe. And that was exactly the point. It was so tight that Pratley would never be able to tug his shirt in a million years. Even if he tried, there just wasn't enough material.

Jamie looked down at his faded old Brazil shirt and thought back to the first time that he saw it: when the kids playing in the *favela* rushed towards him and when he looked into the small, thin boy's eyes for the first time.

Meanwhile, on the sidelines, Rafael also noted Jamie's change of clothing and it had given him his own idea.

It was in the middle of the game and the ball was in play but Rafael quickly called Jamie over to talk to him, to give him one final, vital message in the form of two crucial words.

He whispered those two words into Jamie's ear, only for Jamie to turn and look at Rafael as though he completely nuts.

"What are you doing?!" the kids shouted anxiously, aware that, with Jamie off the field, their team was down to four players and Vetterlein could score the golden goal at any moment. "Jamie! Get back on!"

Jamie was still looking questioningly at Rafael and the two words he had said. Doubt was etched across his face.

But the link between the two boys was now like that between a top coach and a star player. Rafael knew exactly what to say to Jamie and when.

Rafael nodded to Jamie and mouthed six more words:

Do it, Jamie. You are ready.

This time Jamie nodded back.

Ginga!

Jamie flicked the ball into the air and drew all of his skill, rhythm and passion into one place. Then he tilted his head back and bounced the ball on his forehead.

Heading the ball in the air as he ran, Jamie skipped past one, two, three of the teachers, who were unable to even attempt a tackle on Jamie because the ball wasn't on the ground for them to contest.

Jamie smiled. He was actually doing it. If only Mestre could see him now.

"Wow!" shouted the kids.

"The boy's a genius," said Mike, shaking his head in disbelief at what his grandson was capable of.

The only person in the whole playground who was not shocked by what Jamie was doing was Rafael da Cruz. After all, it was his suggestion.

Jamie was proving his friend right with each step that he took. There was now only Pratley left to beat. Jamie ran on, confident that with the ball on his head and his Brazil top too tight to pull, Pratley had no possible way of stopping him.

Jamie remembered how Pratley doubted his ability earlier in the school year and how much it hurt him.

Ginga! Jamie roared in his head as a danced past Pratley. That's what I have that other players don't: *ging*—

Jamie suddenly felt a sharp stab of pain spear into the back of his left ankle. Before he could turn to see what it was, he was tumbling helplessly, face first, into the ground.

To gasps of shock and concern from the crowd, Jamie smacked his chin with dangerous force directly on to the cement and immediately sensed the warm trickle of blood ooze from the wound.

Very quickly, he understood what happened. Pratley wasn't able to pull his shirt, so, instead, he took Jamie down the only way he knew how.

Jamie was now on the ground, writhing in pain with a hole in his chin and no shoe on his left foot.

It was over.

Or at least it would have been for any other player.

Jamie was back up in the blink of an eye, running, with one of his feet completely bare on the rough concrete ground. And yet he felt no pain whatsoever; the hardened outer layer of skin on the sole of his foot was protecting him completely.

He latched back on to the loose ball and touched it once, softly, with his instep. Then, without a second's extra thought, he let go of his strike.

The ball flew off the outside of Jamie's bare left foot, swerving and curling deliciously in the air before bending back in to crash home off the inside of the far post.

Jamie went blank. Everything went silent.

Then, with a rush of noise and with his teammates piling all over him, the world returned.

TEACHERS 3 – 4 STUDENTS
H.VETTERLEIN, 10, 14, 17 J. JOHNSON, 4', 46'

A. CODY, 9'

C. PRATLEY, 40'

STUDENTS WIN WHEATLANDS SCHOOL CUP FOR THE FIRST TIME

Championes, Championes,
Olé, Olé, Olé!

"Well, well, well," said Mr. Karenza.

He was holding a microphone so all the kids, teachers and parents could hear what he was saying. He and the two teams were standing in the middle of the playground, with everyone else watching in a huge circle around them.

"We started this game 11 years ago because we thought that, as the sixth graders prepared to head to middle school, it would be a fun opportunity for them to show their abilities and to go up against the teachers. Well, we obviously had no idea what we were starting!"

The parents all laughed at this comment.

"Each year, the event has grown and the game has become more competitive and, as you know, this is the very first year that the students have won."

All the kids and the parents in the crowd cheered.

"So we wish all of sixth grade the best of luck in middle school and, remember, you can all take what has happened today as a lesson: just because something has never been done before, doesn't mean that it's impossible.

"So our congratulations and the trophy go to the students and their captain, Jamie Johnson. If you'd like to come and collect the trophy, Jamie…"

A huge roar went up around the playground and the kids watching on began to chant once again chant: *"USA! USA! USA!"*

A little embarrassed at all the attention, though equally proud to hear the chant, Jamie walked forward. He wiped his sweaty palms on his old Brazil shirt and shook hands with Mr. Karenza. Then he placed his hands on the gleaming trophy. This was the first real trophy he ever won. It was the trophy he dreamed about lifting for months.

But he knew he could not lift it alone.

"Come on, guys," he shouted to his teammates. "And you too, Rafa! Come and lift it with me!"

It was only when they were all there, all with their hands on the trophy and with all the kids in the playground making the noise of a drumroll, that Jamie and his team finally lifted the prize high into the air.

They were the champions. At last.

The Gift

"I still don't know how we lost it!" Mr. Pratley was saying, shaking his head.

He was sitting down by one of the goals, talking to, or rather at, Gerald Duggins, the only person who was prepared to listen.

The game had finished ten minutes before, and since then, the playground had turned into party central! Jamie, Alex, Rafael, the Talbot Twins, and Aaron Cody were all lifted up into the air, and the other kids gave them fist bumps and high fives.

Then Rafael started playing samba music through his phone and he and Jamie showed everyone how to dance Brazilian style, even Mike joined in. After all, that was his dream: to watch some Brazilian soccer skills and then dance the samba afterwards. He was even dancing with Ms. Vetterlein! The only person who was not enjoying himself was Mr. Pratley. Not only did he lose the big match but Mr. Karenza had decided that the teachers should have a new captain for next year. It was surely going to be Ms. Vetterlein.

"Johnson should have been sent off when he brought me down for the penalty," Pratley moaned, continuing his rant to Mr. Duggins, who was nodding obediently.

"He shouldn't have even been on the field to score the winner. And what was that thing he was doing, bouncing the ball on his head anyway? How are we even supposed to stop that?"

"You can't," said Rafael da Cruz, breaking away from the celebrations. He was standing looking down at Pratley. "That's the whole point."

For a second, Pratley was speechless, stunned by Rafael's confidence. Having devised the special tactics that won the game for the students, the boy with the stutter was now speaking with the confidence of a champion.

"It's called *A Mágica*," Rafael continued.

"*A Mágica*?" a bewildered Pratley repeated. "Where does it come from?"

"You'll have to ask *Foguinho* that," smiled Rafael.

"What are you talking about?" moaned Pratley. "Can you speak English, please? And who on earth is *Foguinho*?!"

"I am," smiled Jamie, joining the conversation.

As he looked at Mr. Pratley, Jamie remembered something that Mike told him not so long ago, something about what you should do when you win.

"Well played, Mr. Pratley," said Jamie. "You're a really good defender and it was a tough battle against you!"

Mr. Pratley turned and stared at Jamie. The man looked as though he never received a compliment before in his life.

"Yes, well," said Mr. Pratley. "Maybe there's a little bit more to your game than kick and chase."

Jamie looked at Mr. Pratley. Did he just hear him right? Did Pratley just say something almost nice to him? Then suddenly something else clicked in Jamie's head. When he joined the conversation between Pratley and Rafael, he was positive that Rafael was speaking without a stammer in public. Could it be? As if to answer the question, Rafael looked at Jamie and reached out his hand.

"Here, Jamie," he said in a clear, confident voice.

Rafael was handing Jamie his notepad.

"I can look at it?" Jamie asked.

"No," said Rafael, shaking his head. "You can keep it."

"No way," said Jamie immediately. "There's no way I can keep it."

Rafael nodded with a warm smile.

"It's yours," he said, placing the notepad into Jamie's hand.

Jamie gently accepted the notepad. He knew better than anyone how much this little book meant to Rafael and how many hours he spent pouring all of his soccer knowledge and ideas into it. With hands slightly trembling, Jamie opened it.

On the first page was written:

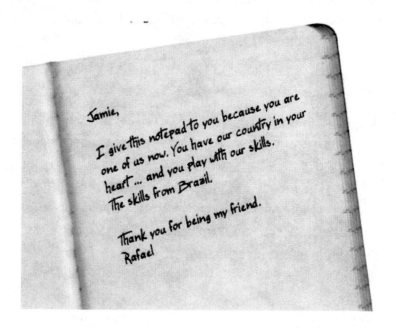

Jamie,

I give this notepad to you because you are one of us now. You have our country in your heart ... and you play with our skills.
The skills from Brazil.

Thank you for being my friend.

Rafael

There were other people starting to gather around Jamie and Rafael now but it made no difference to Rafael's speech; he still carried on speaking freely.

"I don't need it anymore, Jamie," he said. "Thank you for helping me find my voice."

Rafael and Jamie smiled at each other.

They were two soccer geniuses. Of a different kind.

Play On

Saturday, August 23rd – five weeks later

Bernard rested his hand lightly on Rafael's shoulder. It was very nearly time for them to go. The plane was due to take off in half-an-hour.

Jamie knew that he would miss Rafael. Everything that they experienced over the past few months had bonded them together so closely.

After the Teachers vs. Students game and the end of the school year, they spent every day of summer vacation together, back in their favorite old routine: going to the park with Alex and the others until it got dark and then home to Jamie's to rule the world together on Soccer Manager. There wasn't a team on earth that could stop them.

Mike, who brought Jamie to the airport to say goodbye, gave Bernard a firm handshake and Jamie saw that, once again, Bernard was smiling. Since Rafael overcame his stutter after the match at school, Bernard looked as though the weight of the world had lifted from his shoulders. Jamie recognized the smile too; it was just like the one in the photo in his house back in Brazil.

"Last call for Flight 2410 to Rio de Janeiro," boomed the airport announcer.

The boys knew their time was nearly up.

"Keep practicing *A Mágica*!" said Rafael, putting his arm around Jamie after they high-fived. "I can't wait to tell Mestre you actually did it!"

"I will!" replied Jamie. "And if you see Arnaldo, say hi to him and tell him I'm going to be a professional one day, just like him. I really believe it now."

"Me too, Jamie," said Rafael. "And don't worry, I'll be following your career every step of the way."

Both Bernard and Rafael gave Jamie a final wave. Then they slowly turned to walk through the departure gate.

Jamie waved back. His body was completely filled with a feeling of warmth. He imagined Rafael going back to Brazil, speaking without a stutter and starting to build a new future with his dad. Jamie was so proud to have played his part.

But just as he considered that thought, another question jumped rapidly into Jamie's mind: in all the time that he spent with Rafael, who, really, was helping who?

"Rafael!" Jamie shouted, just before they disappeared.

Rafael turned around.

"*Obrigado*," said Jamie, holding up Rafael's notepad. He now carried it with him everywhere, just as Rafael did when he first joined the school.

Rafael's big, Brazilian smile shone back at him.

"Play on, *Foguinho*," said Rafael. His voice rang out clear and true. "Play on…"

Postscript

25 years later

A press conference is being held at Hawkstone United's stadium.

A sharply dressed man walks through the door and into the room. It is full of photographers and journalists all there to hear what he has to say.

The man sits down at the table and clears his throat. He knows what he is going to say. He prepared these words all of last night. He has been preparing for this moment his entire life.

He pulls the microphone towards him and begins to speak.

"I want to say what an honor it is to be managing in the Premier League and, in particular, here at Hawkstone United," he explains.

His voice is cool, crisp, clear and confident.

"This, for me, is a dream come true."

A sea of hands rise into the air. All the journalists want to ask him a question. The man points to a reporter in the third row.

"You've already won trophies in Brazil, Portugal and Spain, and we're delighted to have you in the Premier League now," the journalist says. "But you are the most wanted young manager in the world. You could have picked any club you liked. So why, of all the clubs in the world, have you picked Hawkstone United?"

The man smiles. A big, Brazilian smile.

"Because for me, this club, this place, feels like home," says Rafael da Cruz. "In many ways, my soccer journey started here when I was a kid. And you are right, I did have many offers from many other clubs, but when I discussed it with my wife, Rosária, and I told her that Hawkstone was the club in my heart, we decided I had to take this offer. In the end, it was the only decision we could make."

A door opens at the back of the room, and for a second, all of the photographers and cameras turn to face the phenomenal soccer player who just walked in. But Jamie Johnson is not there to steal the attention; he just wants to watch and listen like everyone else.

"And of course, there is one other very special reason that I had to take this job," Rafael da Cruz says, acknowledging the new arrival. "As a coach, you simply don't turn down the opportunity to work with a player like Jamie Johnson."

Rafael smiles and nods towards the back of the room. Jamie Johnson, captain of Hawkstone United, is smiling too. He gives his old friend and new manager a big thumbs up. Time has passed but their connection is still there. It will always be there.

"Since we were kids, I have followed Jamie's career every step of the way," says Rafael. "How he has never given up, how he has fought back from his horrendous injuries to become the greatest player in this club's history.

"And now, together, with him as my captain, we are about to write a new chapter in Hawkstone's history. And I hope it will be the most exciting chapter of all.

"Jamie Johnson is the man to lead and inspire my new team because he plays the game exactly how I believe it should be played: with skill, with freedom, with passion and with, if I may say, that little touch of magic…"

TOP TEN QUESTIONS
with D.C. Freedman

1. If I have only read *School of Skill*, which Jamie Johnson book should I read next?

Well, *School of Skill* is only the second book in The Jamie Johnson Series, so you have quite a bit to go! I'd recommend starting with *Born to Play*, which is the first book in the series. But remember, it's just the beginning!

2. Do you get much fan mail from your readers?

Yes, with Facebook, Twitter, my website, emails and letters, there are lots of ways for Jamie Johnson fans to get in touch with me and I always make sure I respond. Being an author, you tend to spend a fair bit of time writing on your own, so hearing from people who have read the books is always a brilliant moment. It makes all the hard work worth it!

What was it like writing about Jamie when he was at school?

It was great. At one stage, even the best players in the world—people like Messi and Ronaldo—were just soccer-mad school kids! So we can all empathize with Jamie's dream of making it to the top. Starting Jamie's journey to greatness with him being at school is fun for me as an author too because I already know what happens to Jamie next.

3. Did you do any research about Brazil before you started writing?

I read lots of books about Brazil, its culture and its soccer history. It's such a fascinating country and its soccer history is so rich that it was a treasure trove of information and superb stories. I'm the same as Jamie: slightly obsessed with Brazilian soccer. The Jamie Johnson books are getting quite popular in Brazil now too, which makes me very proud!

4. So is *A Mágica* a real skill and is it allowed in a game?

Yes and yes! I always try to include a special skill in The Jamie Johnson Series and I wanted this one to be particularly unique, as Jamie learns it in Brazil, at Mestre's school of skill! So when I found this skill on the Internet, I knew it was the one. It's mostly called the Seal Dribble because it involves the player balancing the ball on their head like a seal. Check it out on the Internet – it's amazing!

5. What's the best goal you've ever seen?

Marco van Basten's bicycle kick for Ajax vs. Den Bosch in 1986. It's the perfect combination of athleticism, skill and accuracy. If you've read *Born To Play*, you might remember I refer to that goal when Jamie is learning how to do the bicycle kick himself. It's an absolutely brilliant goal; check it out on YouTube!

6. **What's your favorite thing about writing the Jamie Johnson stories, and who is Jamie based upon in real life?**

I get to sit and daydream about soccer! That's my job! I also find Jamie very intriguing as a character. I always say that, with Jamie, you're never quite sure what he's going to do. Is he going to turn around, produce a sensational bit of skill and belt one in from 35 yards? Or is he going to lose his temper, do something he regrets and get himself sent off? Characters like that keep you guessing, which is great for the readers and the author.

Jamie is partly based on me (we have a fair amount in common) and partly based on the great players I have been lucky enough to meet, people like Ronaldo, Beckham, Messi and Rooney. I have taken a little bit from each of these players, added them to my own character and experiences and the result is Jamie Johnson. He is the kind of player I would love to see play live.

7. Which part of *School of Skill* did you most enjoy writing?

I loved Jamie's Brazilian nickname, *Foguinho*: Little Fire. This was suggested to me by a Brazilian friend of mine who I worked with at the FIFA Fustal World Cup. Because it came from a Brazilian soccer expert, I knew I had to use it! I also loved writing about the friendship between Jamie and Rafael, which grew during the story and how it helped give Rafael the confidence to speak freely. Even though I wrote the story and knew what was going to happen, I still felt moved at the end.

8. If you had to pick any soccer player to kick around with, who would it be?

Good question. I have a ton of respect for Steven Gerrard. He offered me his support when I was a completely unknown author in the UK, and I'll never forget that. Thierry Henry is a man full of charisma and intelligence. Maradona, Pelé, Cruyff, Zidane, Best and Charlton are some of the greatest players in the history of the game.

Messi and Ronaldo are both taking soccer to a new level. But perhaps, at the moment, I would like to have a kick around with Gareth Bale. He's a left winger, like Jamie, and there are lots of similarities between their stories too, so I have a ton of questions I need to ask him! Oh, and a game of footvolley with Neymar on the beach on Brazil would be pretty cool too!

9. What the best game you've ever seen live?

I was lucky enough to watch the World Cup Quarter-Final: Brazil vs. England in Japan in 2002 and then fly home on the plane to London with the England players afterwards. I'll never forget it...

From
Rafael's
Notepad ...

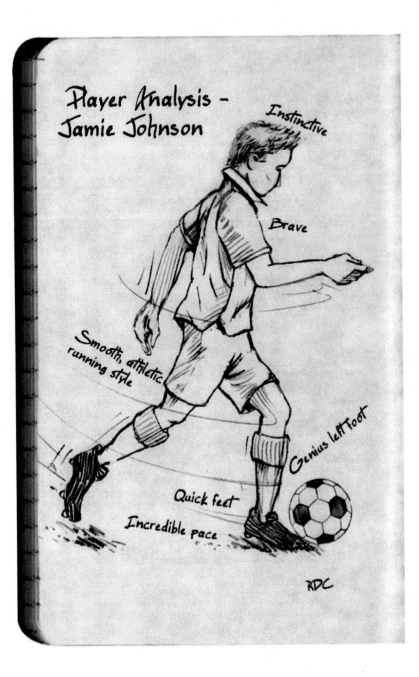

Strengths

- Quick feet
- Incredible pace
- Brave
- Great finisher
- Never gives up
- Smooth, athletic running style
- Eager to learn
- Passionate
- Superb balance
- Unique acrobatic ability
- Instinctive
- Genius left foot
- Potential to be best young player I have ever seen

Weaknesses

- Short temper
- Impatient
- Lack of emotional control
- Doesn't like being told what to do
- Does he know how good he is?

Mestre's A Mágica

Flick the ball up, keep eyes on the ball. Prepare to cushion the ball.

RDC

As forehead cushions the ball, knees bend, back arches. Head moves up in order to keep the ball in position.

Make sure the ball is balanced on top of the forehead. Run with the ball, tilting the head. Keep consistent speed.

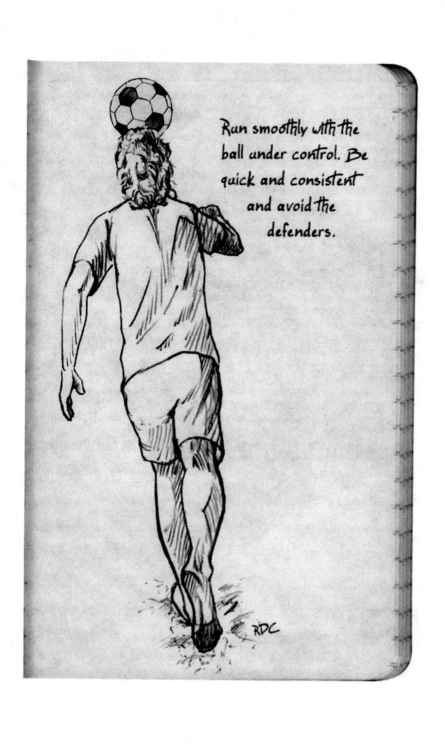

Run smoothly with the ball under control. Be quick and consistent and avoid the defenders.

Speaking Soccer in Brazil!

English	Brazilian/Portuguese
Soccer	Futebol
Ball	Bola
Shot	Chute
Goal	Gol
Skill	Habilidade
Dribble	Finta
Bicycle kick	Bicicleta
Back-heel	Calcanhar
Nutmeg	Caneta
Celebration	Comemoração
Attacker	Atacante
Striker	Centro-avante
Defender	Defensor
Midfielder	Meio-Campo
Goalkeeper	Goleiro
Manager	Gerente
Team	Time
Referee	Árbitro
Free kick	Cobrança de Falta
Foul	Falta
Volley	Voleio
Header	Cabeçada
Cross	Cruzamento (noun)
	Cruzar (verb)
Offside	Impedimento
Whistle	Apito

English	Brazilian/Portuguese
Substitute	Reserva
Stadium	Estádio
Coach	Técnico
Pitch	Campo
Players	Jogadores
Penalty	Penalti
Corner	Escanteio
Throw on	Lateral
Goal kick	Tiro de meta
Half-time	Intervalo
Full time	Final de jogo
Pass	Passe
Score a goal	Fazer o gol
Through ball	Passe em profundidade
Yellow card	Cartão amarelo
Red card	Cartão vermelho
Header	Cabeceio
Net	Rede
Trophy	Troféu
Champions	Campeões
League	Liga
World Cup	Copa do Mundo
Losers	Perdedores
Winners	Vencedores
School of Skill	Escola de Habilidade